AGATHA

BY THE SAME AUTHOR

The Blackmailer
A Man of Power
The Great Occasion
Statues in a Garden
Orlando King
Orlando at the Brazen Threshold

AGATHA

Isabel
Colegate

THE BODLEY HEAD

LONDON   SYDNEY

TORONTO

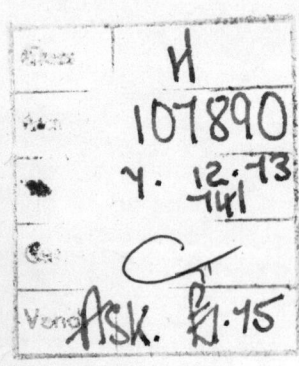
© Isabel Colegate 1973
ISBN 0370 01491 X
Printed in Great Britain for
The Bodley Head Ltd
9 Bow Street, London WC2E 7AL
by W & J Mackay Limited, Chatham
Set in 'Monotype' Imprint
First published 1973

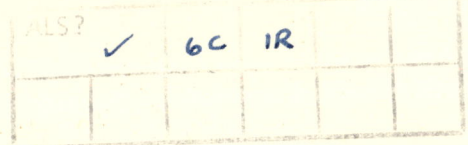

AUTHOR'S NOTE

For those who have not read the earlier books in this trilogy (and even for those who have) it may be helpful to explain that in *Orlando King* Orlando, the illegitimate son of Leonard, was adopted by a Cambridge don, King, a former tutor of both parents, who became a recluse and lived on a remote island in Brittany, where Orlando was brought up. In 1931, at the age of twenty-one, Orlando was sent on a visit to London, and stayed there when his guardian died.

King had given him an introduction to Leonard, though without mentioning their relationship, and Leonard employed him in the furniture factory in Somerset of which he was chairman. Encouraged to a certain extent by Leonard and to a much greater extent by Conrad, the powerful brother of Leonard's wife Judith, Orlando quickly achieved worldly success. Leonard's death, unwittingly accelerated by Orlando, left him free to marry Judith, with whom he had fallen in love. Conrad's patronage helped him to achieve success in politics during the thirties. He was a Cabinet Minister when war broke out in 1939.

The collapse of his marriage to Judith, which culminated in her nervous breakdown, together with what he felt to be his misdirection in politics, led him to resign his public positions and, not being passed fit enough for the armed services, to become an ARP warden during the bombing of London in 1940. As the result of an act of foolhardy courage during a raid, he narrowly escaped death and was left partially blind. Handing over the care of his two daughters to Conrad, he resolved to leave England again as soon as possible and to try to rediscover the life he had led with old King.

In *Orlando at the Brazen Threshold* Orlando was visited in Tuscany, where he had settled after the war, by his daughter Agatha, who in 1951 was seventeen. She encouraged his brief return to England, where Conrad hoped to draw him back into politics or business and his stepsons tried to involve him in their struggles for power in what used to be his family firm, which was about to be taken over by Daintry, the property tycoon. Orlando, his mind cleared by his visit to the scenes of his former life, preferred to return to his hillside and to his attempt to live according to the precepts of his guardian.

Coming to understand how sadly old King himself had failed and how much his own love of his daughter and feeling for her friends gave meaning to his way of life, he was more or less reconciled by the time of the death he had long anticipated. When he died he left Agatha at the point of beginning her life with Conrad's son, Henry.

We know the story of course, so nothing need be withheld. Orlando died; and Agatha was the first to find him, under the bent pear tree in the full heat of the sun.

If in the course of some delicate exploratory operation a surgeon had touched that part of her brain where those particular moments were stored they would have recurred to her with a clarity which patients who have experienced it have described as quite different from the normal action of memory; which seems to show that when five years later Agatha walked, rather quickly because she did not want to be seen, through the woods at Mount Sorrel in the first cold weather of the autumn of 1956 those moments, as well as all the other moments, of her past, though not for the time being present to her conscious mind, were physically contained within her. Her kneeling down beside Orlando on the dry ground which smelt of the herbs he had crushed by his fall, together with the powerful emotion of those first minutes before Nella and Giuseppe came, the clarity, excitement and, it had seemed, unlimited love, were in some minute but scientifically factual way a part of her physical being. As were, presumably, of Conrad's, his distant Indian mornings.

She looked down at Mount Sorrel from the trees at the end of the valley. He was already at his desk in the library writing about India. The house faced her across the park. She did not much like its cold façade—her memories of it, immediate or more distant, were mixed and not pre-

1

dominantly happy—but it had a place in the landscape there, the valley folded to accommodate it, the village clustered behind it and the distance beyond framed it in an eighteenth-century landscape; one which for the moment seemed mostly in tones of grey, except for the low white mist which lay on the floor of the valley concealing the stream. The house was higher than the bed of the stream—lawns sloped down in front of it—and the light on Conrad's desk could be seen from the opposite hillside.

Surprised that he should be up so early, she turned back into the wood and began to walk quickly uphill away from the open valley. Perhaps he did get up early now, old people after all needed less sleep than younger ones, and he was sixty-six this year. She was no longer familiar with the daily routine of his life: she had stayed at Mount Sorrel only once since her marriage. He had leased them a little damp cottage in the woods which had belonged to old Glass the gamekeeper, who was dead now. Conrad very seldom came to see them and probably did not know or care whether or not they were there this particular weekend; or did she only assume his indifference to suit her own purposes, because she distrusted him, had too much to conceal from him, who was after all her husband's father and her own uncle? She had better concentrate on what she had to do.

'Dora?' she called quietly. 'Dora!'

It was a morning for only getting through, for plodding through the fallen leaves with a purpose, not expecting that on this grey day the woods should turn beautiful, as they had been for the past few weeks when there had been sun through slight mist and a haze of cobwebs over every-thing, even, pattern on pattern, sunlight through dew-whitened cobwebs on old man's beard, on hazel or thorn, and the smell of damp leaves; but now she must not be late and must call Dora too from time to time, who had

2

provided her with an excuse for being up so early, should she be required to give one, by getting lost the night before.

She hoped the dog might come dashing down some ride to greet her, was conscious in fact of grey (like the morning) anxiety because Dora was not yet a year old and had never before been out all night, but she had something else to do before she could concentrate on looking for her, and even as she thought of traps, or rabbit-holes, or roads, she had to hurry on to the appointed place: only, passing as she had to do by the entrance to Wood Hill, she could at least turn in there—it was a short cut to where she had to go—and skirting the back of the garden, keeping to the trees, see if there was anything to be seen of the vile seducer, the ugly brute she suspected of being behind the disappearance, the utterly appalling Sandy.

The house, Wood Hill, where she had spent the first eight years of her life, was still shuttered and curtained against the night. There was an elderly couple living there now: not much was known about them except that they were the owners of an unpleasant undisciplined dog. There had been children once but they had grown up and gone. Agatha waited for a moment, concealed in the trees. Would Dora, an early riser, scratch at a door, bark? There was no sound and she turned to go. Unexpectedly a door opened. He emerged, sniffed the ground, a yellow dog, cross between a labrador and something smaller, nastier, a hyena perhaps; bristly along the back as if his hackles were always up, little eyes, unnecessary whiskers; and alone. The door shut behind him.

Agatha moved as quietly as she could through the trees and over the top of the hill. She heard him bark, but half-heartedly. He was not even a good watch-dog.

Her anxiety was now acute, but she must not be late.

Conrad wrote, 'My father was very distressed by Lord

3

Curzon's resignation. He felt that the Government at home had completely failed to understand the grandeur of Curzon's concept of Empire. But by that time I had been sent home to school.'

Seven, his life the heat and smell of India, parakeets, flying foxes, brilliant red flowers in darkest deodar trees, soft rain on early morning rides over the foothills of the Himalayas, sounds and smells of the camp, following his father as he dispensed justice. At school he would learn to be wise, good and immeasurably grand, like his father. The untouchable was his mother's smell in some kind of soft drapery which covered her warmth as she kissed him goodbye. It was as if they had cut off his arm and said, 'Grow another to prove yourself worthy.' The memory was stored away somewhere, part of him but not to be recalled, though he could remember very clearly the feel and smell of his pony Sam. His father had represented to him that owning meant being dedicated to serve. He had honoured his father and mother and in the sweet-scented Indian morning had cantered along mountainous paths followed by his faithful syce.

Conrad wrote in his memoirs, 'I have very happy memories of my childhood in India.'

Over the top of the hill there was a plantation of conifers, only a few years old and too thick to walk through. Agatha followed the fence round the edge of it and joined a track leading downhill, into the small valley in which were the ruins of the old Timberwork factory. The part that still stood was the eighteenth-century stone structure, roofless now, which had been built as a paper mill. The additions which had been made in the nineteen-thirties, when Orlando had been turning the little furniture factory into the highly profitable organisation it had later become, had collapsed now and lay in heaps of rubble, encroached

4

upon by willow herb. Through the tall trees beyond she could see the viaduct which took the railway line across the narrow valley. Here again there was a lurking mist; the trees emerged through it with an effect almost of a Chinese landscape, the occasional huge conifer dark among the elms and hornbeams.

She took an overgrown path halfway down the hill and crossed the hillside parallel to the stream until she reached a point from which she could look down through the trees to where the road curved under the tall arch of the viaduct. Here a car had drawn up on the grass verge. There was a thermos flask on its roof and the three men standing near were holding mugs. Two of the men were wearing hats and rather long belted overcoats; the other, who was standing a little apart from them, was Agatha's half-brother Paul, a convicted traitor.

He looked a good deal smaller than the other two, hatless and wearing over the navy-blue suit he had worn at his trial a short duffle coat bought from a government surplus store, originally more or less white, but dirty now. His shoulders were bent and both hands were clasped round his cup as if to keep them warm.

Agatha walked slowly towards them down the hill, her hands in her pockets, reluctant to reach the moment when he must look up and see her. The sound of her own gumboots against her legs—a sound she usually liked because of its agreeable associations—seemed loud to her as she approached, but none of the three men looked in her direction. She was almost out of the trees and onto the grass before Paul saw her, said 'Ah!', put down his mug on the bonnet of the car, and came up to put his hands on her arms and kiss her quickly on both cheeks.

The men in hats hardly glanced at her. It crossed her mind that they might have been aware of her approach all the time.

Gesturing vaguely in their direction, Paul said as if in introduction, 'Bill and Ben, the flowerpot men,' and with a hand on her arm led her away from them to the other side of the car.

'It worked all right then?' said Agatha.

'Yes. Thank you.'

'I'm glad you've got some coffee,' said Agatha, rather quickly. 'I was going to bring some but then I thought I'd be sure to wake the children.'

'Have some.'

'Is there time?'

'Of course, come on,' said Paul, but as he reached for the thermos he shot a quick glance towards the two men, and she realised with a slight shock that he was frightened of them. She tried a polite smile in their direction—*she* was not a criminal after all—and one of them nodded back. Perhaps it was the one who had come to see her to ask her for the money for the escape. She was not quite sure because of the hat, but it could have been the same; he had the same look of consciously assumed anonymity, as if all sorts of other expressions might cross his face when he was not on the job. She thought he seemed efficient and reliable—always assuming that one was on the same side— and was annoyed with Paul for being frightened of him.

'You know you could get five years for this,' said Paul.

Agatha, who had not realised the penalty was so great, although she had known—in spite of having temporarily forgotten it—that in fact she indeed was a criminal too, paused for a moment before answering. Then she said, very calmly, 'What a lot.'

'Oh yes,' said Paul as if he found the idea obscurely satisfying. 'Helping a criminal escape from prison. Very serious offence.'

Agatha looked at him, finding his mood, as so often, hard to gauge.

6

'What weak coffee,' she said.

'Hot though.'

'Where will you go?'

'You'd better not know. They'll keep me somewhere for a bit before they get me out of the country. It's safer that way. I'll send you a message when I get there. We could probably meet somewhere or other.'

He said it without conviction. Everything about him except his businesslike suit seemed pale: the grubby duffle coat, the thin face, slightly greasy in complexion, the fair hair, shorter than usual (had they cut it in prison?), the eyes avoiding hers, light blue eyes whose gaze in better times had sometimes been dazzling. The word 'desolation' came into her head, at the same time as the thought that he had no one but her.

'We must,' she said. 'We must meet somehow.'

He turned away a little.

'I don't know where I'll be.'

'Tell them to let me know when you're safely out of the country. They can do that somehow or other, can't they? Otherwise I shan't know when you're safe.'

'O.K.'

'And then you send me a message. I'm always here.'

But he was fumbling in the pockets of the duffle coat, bringing out a packet of cigarettes, extracting one with difficulty because his hands were trembling violently. 'Even now?' he asked with the cigarette in his mouth, as he grappled with the matchbox.

'Of course even now.'

'But you don't—' He had managed to light the cigarette, and paused to draw on it deeply. 'You don't approve of what I've done.'

'Of course I don't approve of what you've done. I think it was an awful thing to do. But I've often not approved of you.'

He nodded, half smiled; but she noticed with horror a tear trickling down the side of his nose.

'Paul, listen, get through these next few days, do what they tell you. Here, I've got a bit of money, take it. Get them to buy you books so you don't get depressed, hiding. And then when you get there, Paul, have a nice time, do.'

He looked at her questioningly.

'No, it's important. Don't have guilt and all that, it's such a bore. Have a nice time. You know—those things you like—drink, and boys and things.'

He shook his head, but giggled weakly, looked at her again, and laughed outright.

'Well, you know—' said Agatha, smiling reluctantly.

'What a business,' he said, shaking his head again. 'What a lark, what an episode.'

'Work would be the best thing of course,' said Agatha, relieved to see his spirits improving. 'And your money might run out soon, mightn't it? Can't you write a book, Paul? You're much cleverer than most people who do.'

'A travel book?' he suggested ironically.

'Yes, a travel book, why not? They're what everyone reads these days. There's a new thing, just started, I read about it somewhere, a Book Club just for travel books. That shows. . . . Oh do, Paul, and send it to me and I'll find a publisher and make all the arrangements and everything.'

'I might.'

'Do.'

'How are the children?' he asked quickly. Each was as nervous as the other that there might be a gap in the conversation.

'All right.' Beginning to smile, she added, 'Very well in fact.'

'And that awful beagle?'

'She's not awful.'

8

'You'll never be able to keep her in London.'

'Of course I will!'

He shook his head. 'Too boisterous. You won't be able to control her.' He sounded pleased again, as he had at the thought of her going to prison for helping him.

She did not answer.

'And our dear uncle?' he asked, his hard ironical tone not concealing from her his anxiety to know how Conrad was bearing the shame.

'Very busy I think,' she said.

'Starting a war, I suppose.'

'No, he doesn't seem particularly belligerent. If you mean about Egypt. Not that he's exactly *un*belligerent. I don't know what he thinks really. He's starting to write his memoirs.'

'Good Lord, I never thought he'd do that. Early days, Eton and Oxford, and all that?'

'I suppose so.'

'Perhaps that's what I should write. My memoirs.'

'Could you?'

'No. No, I couldn't. They'd be a pack of lies, wouldn't they?'

The men in overcoats were moving, one merely shifting from foot to foot to keep warm, the other approaching the car with two mugs. They watched him open the car door, bend to put the mugs inside, straighten up again to reach out for the thermos.

'Look here,' said Paul hurriedly, taking her by the elbow to turn her slightly away from the car. 'I've got more money than you think. I'll be all right. You'd better go now. I'll send you a message. Give my love to Henry and the children. Tell Henry to buy Logan shares if he can raise some money. They'll recover. Daintry's still the hottest operator in the business.'

'I will give them your love,' said Agatha. 'Later I

9

mean. I'd better not now.'

'No, quite right. Keep your mouth shut. Now don't worry, will you?'

'No.'

'I'd better go then.'

The men were waiting by the car, one with his hand on the handle of the door by the driver's seat. This one's face had assumed a rather more amiable expression; perhaps he was relieved that they were about to move on.

'O.K.?' he asked.

The other one was getting into the back seat.

'Yes, yes, here we are, off we go,' said Paul fussily.

The driver took his seat, shutting the door quietly. Paul kissed Agatha quickly on the cheek and got in beside him, winding down the window. When he had shut the door he lent out and said, 'Don't forget, get hold of some Logan shares. You'll be on to a good thing.'

She nodded, raised a hand. The car started. Paul waved and smiled and the wind blew his pale hair away from his face as the car moved off. She thought he looked younger than thirty-five. She waited by the road. The sound of the car faded. The sky was lighter; there might be some sun after all. A very slight breeze stirred the trees behind her. Leaves fell, and a chestnut hit the damp earth.

'I have no money,' said Agatha aloud, as if she were patiently explaining. 'Because I spent what I had and a good deal more on getting you out of prison.'

Perhaps it was an exaggeration—pushed to extremes, there was probably something she could sell—but she could not help minding that none of that seemed to have crossed his mind for a moment: he did take things for granted.

She shook herself slightly, as if she had been wet, and began to walk rapidly along the road in the opposite direction to that in which the car had gone; having now no need of concealment, she could walk back by road and hope to find Dora on the way, or if not on the way then back at the cottage, for she might just possibly have spent the night in shelter somewhere and come home at daylight. Or she might have gone to Mount Sorrel—that was a new idea, quite hopeful—someone there would certainly have taken her in if it had been late—they would not have been able to let Agatha know because there was no telephone at the cottage—and Conrad would walk up with her before breakfast, with his fat old labrador—he would not have come earlier even though, as she knew, he had been awake, because he would have thought they would still be asleep, unfamiliar as he was with the early-rising habits of small children. . . . She concentrated on these possibilities, walking rapidly and not thinking about Paul; she would not allow herself to think about Paul; on that subject her mind was tired, nor did she like the prospect of having to admit to herself—and certainly she would never do so to anyone else—that she almost despaired of him.

She passed the ruined mill and followed the track into the woods behind it, approaching the sound of the stream. Earlier in the autumn the track had been very muddy but now after the first few frosts of winter it was easier to walk on. It led her past the waterfall and through the darkest part of the wood, where the trees were tallest and the valley steepest, and out into a field made muddy by the bullocks who looked up at her curiously, their breath steaming from their nostrils, and through another rough little copse out onto the road which passed Wood Hill and went on into the village, and turning a corner on this road she saw Dora and turned back at once, stood on the grass verge, waited, pressed her hands against her face. Certainly the dog must be dead.

Agatha walked up and down on the grass as if by refusing to go round the corner again she could deny what lay beyond, which was Dora dead by the roadside, killed by a car. Fighting with the information, she heard a car in the distance. It was coming up the hill, must be passing the dog now, came round the corner, a Land-Rover with a man driving it who slowed down. Stiff, her hands in her pockets, she was frozen in fear that he might stop; until, catching a glimpse of her face, he accelerated, embarrassed, there being nothing he could do.

'It's only a dog after all,' said Agatha firmly and walked round the corner.

Dora lay by the edge of the road, apparently unmarked. Her limpness showed her to be dead, but her compact little body looked otherwise unchanged and her coat, which had seemed as if it must have been polished with silk, though it was only youth and health which made it shine, was upspoilt: even people who had found her too energetic or who didn't like dogs had admitted she was beautifully marked: only a fleck of blood by her mouth: it seemed such a pity.

Beside her on the grass was a piece of paper, torn from the back of a book. Agatha picked it up. On it was written in pencil, 'Sorry about this little foxhound, jumped out very fast and killed at once. There was another dog but he ran off.' Sandy the murderer. Looking up, she saw the blood on the road. She could only have failed to see it before because her eyes had been fixed on the corpse—a great bright scarlet splash down the middle of the pale grey road, oh she'd spilt her blood all right, and Agatha began to sob, crumpling the note in her hand, momentarily overwhelmed by love and admiration. She'd stood on a hillside, autumn bright on the long grass with low yellow sunshine and Dora had scented sheep, being unfamiliar with them, and from right across the big field—she below Agatha on one side, the sheep on the other, grazing—had begun to give chase. Her firm deep-chested body built for speed, tail for once a backward-bending curve, she bounded through the tall grass as the silly sheep began to fluster, hustled together, ran, the sound of their matted pelts against their legs possibly intoxicating to a pursuer. Agatha shouted—why should she obey?—but without slackening her pace a moment she came in a great bounteous sweep of movement to her feet as if, running so beautifully, it made no difference to her where she ran. And so she'd dashed at death like that and spouted all her warm bright blood onto the road.

Agatha crouched to pick up the limp body, head against hers, then carried it to the edge of the wood by the road. She would return later with a spade to bury it, but in the meantime, unaware that there was now an observer among the trees behind her, she covered the body with fallen leaves.

'We can only bleed,' she said.

The familiar tone, calmly authoritative, as if precise diction could conceal its sadness, came to the man watching her. He turned away, moving quickly back through the trees the way he had come.

Agatha knelt on the damp ground, piling high the dead leaves.

Conrad wrote with a relief nib, smoothly and fast, in a firm Palmerstonian hand. The task bored him. He found that speech was a much more natural means of communication than this remote refined process of thought, manual labour and solitude. He was not a voluble man but had spent a lifetime working for various aims by means of verbal persuasion, whether at private talks or public meetings. He was used to the action and reaction involved, and without it found the writer's task too unresponsive, in a sense perhaps too arrogant; there was no interplay of personality, no way of gauging an audience's reaction or bending to it. How much should he describe of India in the 1890s? There was no listening face whose expression could tell him the answer. Was that life—on tour, in Simla, in Delhi—of interest to anyone nowadays?

'There's rather a vogue for travel books,' he said, frowning and wondering whether it was time for breakfast. But the Empire was out of fashion. 'It will come back of course,' he said, beginning to address an imaginary audience of attentive youth, 'because it's a very interesting subject. The life that was led, the type of individual that was produced to wield these huge responsibilities, to live this life of in some ways enormous self-sacrifice and in others extraordinary fulfilment, all this will be seen in due course to be uniquely fascinating. Uniquely fascinating.'

Should he describe Government House, Calcutta, modelled on Kedleston, its fantastic gardens, the Viceroy's bodyguard, his Indian servants in their scarlet livery with the Viceregal monogram embroidered in gold? Instead he wrote, 'I am far from nostalgic. I had always said that Independence must come, and was one of the people working to see that it came sooner rather than later. Of course I regret many things about the manner of its coming, the bloodshed, the Labour Government's precipitance. . . .'

'I'd have liked to have done it myself of course,' he said slowly, putting down his pen. 'I'd have liked to have stage-managed the handover myself.' He smiled indulgently at his own vanity.

The telephone rang. Apologies. Was he in bed?

'No, no, just doing a bit of writing. Otherwise I'd have been in Church. Dodging it this morning, I'm ashamed to say.'

The Prime Minister wanted an extra Cabinet meeting— 'Of course, yes, tell him I'll be there.'

Putting down the receiver, he said, 'Hope the silly fool

knows what he's doing,' disrespectfully but without real anxiety.

Henry walked back through the wood to the cottage. It was small and yellow-washed with wooden lattice work round the roof of a pointed gable, a seaside boarding-house in a forgotten Victorian resort rather than a gamekeeper's cottage. He pushed open the back door and looked into the kitchen where the children were eating cornflakes.

'I'm just going to telephone a minute. You'd better come.'

They looked shocked.

'We haven't finished our breakfast.'

'Where's Mummy?'

'She's just coming. Here, take this.' He cut two pieces of brown bread, put butter and honey on them, and gave one to each child. They took them and climbed into the back of the car.

'I thought we were going to have sausages,' said George.

'We are, when we get back. I didn't want to leave you alone.'

'We'd have been all right,' said George.

'Supposing Lucy had cut her finger?'

'I'd have held it under the cold tap until you came back,' said George.

'She might not have let you, you know what she is.'

'I'd knock her out, and then hold it under the cold tap.'

'I'll knock you out,' said Lucy. 'And chop you in bits and put you down the lavatory. And pull the plug, I will.'

'Don't be silly, Lucy,' said Henry. 'People don't leave people of five and four alone in houses anyway. I don't know why but they just don't. Now I'm going into the telephone-box and you can sit here a minute and if you quarrel I'll be very angry.'

'*You'll* be very angry?' said George loudly. 'You mean

15

we will.' This seemed to strike him as immensely funny and he began to roll around, laughing, in the back of the car.

Henry watched them from the telephone-box and soon Lucy began to wave her hands up and down frantically, making horrible faces. George reached into the front of the car for Henry's coat, searched through the pockets and gave her a handkerchief: she must have had honey on her fingers.

'Sally? Oh I'm sorry, you were asleep.'

'Of course I was asleep, it's very early.'

'I'm sorry. Sally?'

'Mn?'

'I'm sorry.'

'Well, all right then.'

'I wish I was there.'

'Is that what you rang up to say?'

'No. The thing is, Dora—you know, that dog—she's been run over.'

'Oh poor thing. Is she dead?'

'Yes.'

'Is Agatha very upset?'

'Yes. At least I think so.'

'You think so?'

'I haven't spoken to her. I just saw her, picking her up. It must have happened in the night. I came back. Agatha looked so . . . I didn't want to go up to her.'

'Henry, you must. You must go and look after her. Poor Agatha, she really loved that dog. I know what it is. Go on, Henry, go and find her.'

'You're very kind. I will go. The thing is, I may not be able to get away tonight after all, I'll have to see how it goes.'

'Yes, I see.'

'Sally, darling, I'll ring up later.'

16

'I'm going out.'

'I'd better say I'll see you tomorrow night. About nine. Without fail. Sally?'

'Yes?'

'You're very nice.'

'Oh *Henry*.'

'Sorry to be so hopeless. Goodbye, Sally—'

He went out, smiling affectionately, and got into the car. On the way back to the cottage he told the children that Dora had been hit by a car when she was crossing the road, just like the badger who had been killed a few weeks ago, and that they must be very kind to their mother who would be feeling sad about it.

Agatha had become pregnant quite soon after their marriage. It threw her into a relationship of unaccustomed intimacy with her own body: she was embarrassed as well as fascinated, too embarrassed to go to the relaxation classes which her doctor had recommended but fascinated enough to read everything she could find in the Chelsea Public Library on the subject of childbirth, from which she had gleaned the general impression that if having a baby hurt you it was your own fault. Confirming as it did her inclination towards guilt of any kind, this misapprehension left her free to assume, after a last-minute anaesthetic and a forceps delivery, that she was not much good as a natural woman. This might have worried her more than it did had not quite another realisation begun to dawn upon her, which was that through no virtue of her own, for the virtue was all on the other side, she was a good mother.

It appeared to her that George was a perfect organism, requiring only her intelligent co-operation in order to complete his biologically pre-ordained progress. That being so, she could not see her task as a very difficult one; but it did require a certain discipline, a watchfulness in case she should, instead of interpreting, impose. She already had an idea of all loving activity as involving self-restraint, and in this sense her newly discovered and previously unimaginable maternal love seemed of a higher quality than her love for her husband. If love between adults was a process which only began when one's love was returned, it implied two selves, liable to make demands: in maternal love self-abnegation could be complete. Thus she was grateful to George for her first breath of freedom from herself, a breath that at certain of her more ecstatic moments she could imagine might in the course of time prove to have been a first gasp of the great white air of death.

The baby was breast-fed at first. The doctor had pronounced views on feeding. He was a dark-haired young man with a sternly professional air and a kind of restrained fanaticism about social justice, which meant that he accepted no private patients and that Agatha had to sit for a long time in his surgery waiting-room before seeing him. She did this gladly, because she admired him without qualification and had erotic fantasies about him which she allowed to run riot because she had heard that it always happened between maternity patients and their doctors. At one month, cod liver oil and orange juice; at six weeks, mashed banana. Then came yolk of egg, then apple purée, then Farex mixed with cow's milk (at the cottage she boiled this for three minutes in case the milk was not so purified as in London). Rose-hip syrup for sweetening, never sugar. Soon the two o'clock feed consisted of egg-yolk and mashed carrot, fruit and orange juice, and by the time George was two and a half months old he was no longer breast-fed but drank cow's milk from a bottle at his first and last feeds. The method was crowned with success; each meal was a triumph. George grew plump and took on a sort of overall gloss, or sheen, outward manifestation of a superlative mechanism within. He smiled now, and thumped vigorously with his heels on his red kicking rug. From the privacy of his first months of life he emerged, buttoned into a sort of bag with arms, onto the streets of Chelsea in his pram.

She walked the same streets with both of them later.

'Keep away from the road.' 'Wait for me at the edge of the pavement.' '*Stop*, Lucy!' 'Hold my hand to cross the road.' Carrying her shopping basket, always afraid they might be run over.

But when they got to the shops they were still her licence to existence, the experience shared which admitted her to ordinary life—'Oh they *are*, at that age'—and I am one of you, she sometimes thought, saying, 'Two pounds of granulated,' smiling because another child is staring at mine from behind a pile of soup tins. We are the same, we see they get decent meals and have their noses wiped; that is to say, we've knelt, 'Come on, push,' we've said, the plump foot dangling nonchalant, laces to be tied, and been aware of this sometimes as such an act of love as dazzles the imagination. 'Go on then run,' we've said. 'Not too fast, you'll fall; oh you silly little thing, what did I tell you?' So we tire ourselves out, as an arm aches, held for a hawk to fly from.

These feelings expressed themselves only in a smile or two, a word perhaps to a strange child, a standing aside for someone with a heavier basket. She knew very few of her neighbours by name. The street was a poor one, in the course of being transformed into something smarter: the process had not gone far as yet, but there was a property company which owned or was acquiring a good many of the freeholds and was selling long leases after repairing the houses. The milkman had told Agatha that fourteen families had been evicted from two of the houses opposite, which were going to be turned into a vicarage. Agatha had

written to the Vicar, who replied that there was no truth
in the story. He thought her quite mad. Nor was the milkman pleased when she told him; he preferred to believe
the calumny.

Henry gave her coffee, said he would cook the lunch,
offered to go with a spade and bury Dora.

She drank the coffee.

'I have to give her her due, don't I?' she said apologeti-
cally. 'I won't go on about it.'

He reassured her, said she was quite right. He cooked
the children their late breakfast of sausages, dressed them
in their duffle coats and gloves and boots and sent them,
the little shock of Dora's death already easily absorbed
(her claws had always been rather sharp), to play behind
the cottage, where they had made a house in what used to
be an outside privy.

'It's unbelievable, how kind you are,' said Agatha,
moving closer to the fire he'd left.

He kissed her cheek gently. 'I am quite good sometimes,
aren't I?' he said, rather pressing the point.

'Incredibly good.'

'I know you think I'm useless,' he said. 'But did you see
those sausages? A bit split, not at all burnt, perfect. I'm
going to do the lunch too. You're just going to sit there
quite quietly. Papers, do you want? I've got them already.
They're there when you want them. I'm just going to peel
the potatoes now.'

'You won't forget the burying?'

'As soon as I've peeled the potatoes I'm going.'

She could imagine scavenging noses pushing at the soft
flesh.

'It has to be deep. Foxes dig.'

'I know, don't worry.'

'You won't let the children follow you?'

'I'll go out of the front.'

'Thank you very much, Henry.'

He smiled, patted her head, and left.

He walked straight ahead, to keep the cottage between him and the children, and then when he reached the trees turned right and, skirting the road, joined the track he had taken earlier in the morning and which was a short cut to Wood Hill. When he had woken up to find Agatha gone, he had assumed that she had walked to Wood Hill in the hope that Dora might have spent the night there, and he had left the children to start their breakfast and walked in that direction expecting that he might meet her on the way back. He had walked all the way to the road before he saw her kneeling on the ground, piling leaves on the dead dog and saying, 'We can only bleed.'

He knew very well to what she was referring. Her vision was such as to see everything in parallels and correspondences, and he knew that she had in mind not only Dora's death but her own unhappiness as the result of the pain he inflicted on her by his love for Sally, and in reference to which she had once said, 'I only have one reaction. I think I only have one cell. I can only let out an awful black cloud of love like an inkfish when you prod it. I'm not proud of it, it's so useless and tiring. Also, why should I involve you with my entrails? It's an imposition.'

It was not that he did not understand Agatha. He did, a good deal better than she understood him. But he did not know what to do about her.

Agatha's sister Imogen, who was twenty at this time, had certain mannerisms which Agatha found irritating. For instance, when she met Agatha and the children in the street, the day that Agatha had agreed to find £700 to finance Paul's escape from prison and journey to some unknown foreign country, she had swooped down upon Lucy, with jingling bracelets and flying scarves, lifted her high in the air, hugged and kissed her, bent to return her to the pavement and said, 'Instant blissikins.'

George stood watching, rightly (to Agatha's mind) embarrassed. Imogen then kissed him, and said, 'Georgie Porgie, pudding and pie, kissed the girls and made them cry', a rhyme he particularly disliked. In fact, though, he was very fond of Imogen, and responded warmly to her unusual prettiness: he was prepared to accept that there should be, especially at moments of greeting, a certain amount of superficial nonsense to be got through: he even sensed, though he had never thought it out, that there was some kind of initial nervousness involved.

'How's the magazine world?' said Agatha, implying criticism.

'Phoney,' said Imogen, forestalling it.

It was still summer, and she was wearing a yellow dress tightly waisted and full-skirted. She was employed by a fashion magazine, her contributions being mainly towards a column on accessories: a good many of these she sported herself, a thick shiny plastic belt, for instance, two diaphanous yellow chiffon scarves, and the jingling bracelets. She was never still, shook her long fair hair back from her face or tucked wandering strands of it behind her ear, fidgeted with the bracelets, twined the scarves through her fingers, her face meanwhile, even when she was speaking with breathless animation, preserving a kind of absorbed serenity, like a dancer's, inherent perhaps in its own perfect structure.

'Do you know who I met last night?' she said, beginning to walk along the street beside Agatha.

'No?'

'Gary Cooper.'

'What was he like?'

'Fabulous. He asked me to have dinner with him.'

'And did you?'

'Not then. Some time, he meant. He said he'd ring up. Do you think he will?'

'I expect so. I mean, if he said he would. . . .'

'There was this man who'd been in Monte Carlo with him and he had a tummy upset, and he went into the chemist to get some medicine and Prince Rainier came in, and he said, "Hey, Prince, I been throwing up all over your kingdom".'

'Probably he was a friend of his.'

'No, he'd never seen him before. I think.'

'Oh.'

'Well, anyway—'

'Yes, well, how funny. Where was this?'

'Some party. I don't know whose party it was actually. I went with Adrian.'

'Oh yes.'

'He's getting a new flat. It's awfully nice. In Chesham Place.'

'Let's go in down here. The door's open. Careful, Lucy, hold onto the railing.' They went down the steep steps into the area, past the dustbins and through the basement door. The kitchen was at the back, looking out onto a square of garden on its own level. The children went out to dig in the sandpit and Agatha began to unload her shopping basket.

'You'll have lunch, of course.'

'I can't really, I'm supposed to be looking at a whole lot of places in the King's Road.'

'Can't you look at them after lunch?'

'I suppose so. I'm supposed to meet a photographer at two o'clock in a stocking bar.'

'Unless it's a place where you eat stockings you might as well have lunch first. We always have it quite early anyway because Willy comes at two.'

23

'How's all that working?'

'Rather well. She does all sorts of useful things that I've never asked her to do. The children love her. And I like the bookshop.'

'Do they still only pay you three pounds a week?'

'Yes, it isn't very much, is it? Perhaps they'll give me some more at Christmas or something.'

'It's an awful long time until Christmas. Why don't you ask them?'

'They look quite poor. I shouldn't think they make much money out of it.'

'How's Henry's job?'

'Boring, I think, but he seems to be getting used to it.'

'Perhaps he'll get a rise.'

'I think he thinks more in terms of not getting sacked.'

'So do I,' said Imogen with feeling.

'He'll do something quite different one day, and be quite different about it. But I don't know what, or when.'

This was as near as Agatha ever came to discussing her problems with anyone, and the feeling of the nearness, as she sliced tomatoes with a sharp knife, was momentarily worrying, in case she should go further and talk about Sally, which she had never done to anyone except Henry—and not very much even to him—but she did really know that the temptation would pass and that she would be glad not to have succumbed to it, and that anyway after the conversation she would feel as comforted as if they had discussed everything and been mutually reassured. Sliding the knife cleanly through the tomato, she did not hurry to raise the subject of Paul, though she knew she would have to do it before Imogen left.

'There's room for me there,' said Imogen, fiddling with her bracelets.

'Where?' asked Agatha, who was still thinking about Henry.

'In Adrian's new flat,' said Imogen.

Agatha did not pause in her slicing, concealing her reaction, which was negative.

'He wants me to move in,' said Imogen.

'What about when Gary Cooper rings up?' said Agatha.

'That's nothing to do with it,' said Imogen.

'Yes it is. If you're living with someone you're supposed to be their person, aren't you?'

'You don't think it's a good idea.'

'Why don't I ask Henry what he thinks?'

'All right. I can see you're just being tactful, but, yes, ask Henry, I'd like to know what he thinks.'

'Lucy likes cauliflower,' said Agatha. 'And spinach and cabbage and all the things children are supposed to hate.'

'I get so sick of the flat,' said Imogen. 'And I do like Jane and Diana but they get on my nerves sometimes. And it's always so untidy.'

'I don't think that's a serious enough reason for going to live with Adrian.'

'I'm not a very serious person.'

'I know,' said Agatha, putting a saucepan on the stove. 'Why doesn't a millionaire come and marry you?'

'I don't think I'm the sort of person people marry.'

'Rubbish,' said Agatha angrily.

But Imogen was looking down, her hair hanging forward over her face.

'I mean I absolutely wouldn't dream of marrying Adrian,' she said, fiddling with her bracelets. 'But I think in a way he might have asked me, don't you?' Her face screwed up and tears fell softly onto her hands.

'I *hate* him!' said Agatha, stamping her foot.

She turned back to the stove and began to bang saucepans about unnecessarily.

'Yes, well, anyway,' she said, 'I don't really think you should move in with him in that case, and also you know it is entirely your own fault people don't treat you better, you're much too humble. You ought to be nastier. Do try.' Talking to allow Imogen time to recover from her tears, she meanwhile put chops under the grill and mixed oil and vinegar as a dressing for the tomatoes. 'You could do it all so much better if that's the sort of thing you want to do. Look at all the opportunities you missed after those marvellous photographs in *Vogue*. You could be a famous model, a film star or something. What about spending less time with Adrian and more on your job, for instance?'

Imogen was staring dreamily out of the window.

'How can I get people to like me for myself, not for what I look like?' she said.

'Women,' said Agatha, turning the chops. 'What's to be done about them?'

Neither expected an answer.

After a few minutes Agatha felt able to raise the subject of Paul's escape. She and Imogen both had a small income from money left by their father in trust for their children, but they were unable to use the capital. Conrad was their principal trustee and as his belief was that young people should make their own way in the world he was unapproachable on such subjects, as he was also unshakeable in his resolve to give his own only child Henry, whom he considered a wastrel, nothing at all, except the lease of the gamekeeper's cottage at Mount Sorrel, until he had in some sense or other satisfactory to his father proved himself. The raising of a ransom for Paul was therefore not a simple matter.

Imogen was shocked at the suggestion.

'I don't think he ought to be got out,' she said. 'He committed a crime.'

'I know he did. But he's our brother.'

'I thought it was all over. Have we all got to start worrying again?'

26

'We don't have to do the escaping. All we have to do is raise the money.'

'And then what? Does he expect us to look after him?'

'They're going to get him out of the country. That's part of the deal.'

'It's illegal.'

'Of course.'

'I don't want to go to prison.'

'You wouldn't. But think, if you don't want to go to prison, imagine being sent there for fifteen years.'

'He'll get remission, won't he, for good behaviour?'

'You know he'd never survive it. He's not resilient, Paul.'

'Nor was Stephen, was he?'

'What's that to do with it?'

'Paul killed Stephen.'

'You can't say that. No one can ever be blamed for someone else's suicide. It's something in them, I mean in the people who kill themselves. Besides, no one could have expected it. We all thought Stephen really tough, so pompous as he was with us all. But he must have had an inclination that way. After all our mother did.'

'They're only our half-brothers,' said Imogen, shying away from the thought of their mother's death.

'All right then.'

'Well, Agatha, I really don't think you should. I mean if people break the law, they have to pay the penalty.'

'That's not what I think,' said Agatha. 'Not everybody. Not every law.'

'You surely don't suggest that the law was wrong?'

'Of course not. But the law has its sphere, its role. There are other spheres, and other roles.'

'I don't understand you.'

'It doesn't really matter.'

She had been walking along in Bath once, on an afternoon when it had been raining and had then brightened towards evening, so that the sun which lit the wet street wa low and took the passers-by from the side casting long shadows; and the people, buildings, cars and pigeons took on an unaccustomed gleaming significance, as if they had been in a film and Agatha had read the reviews and knew there was going to be a bank robbery; or, rather, as if something had already happened, something which they all knew about and which was going to change the world.

During the few moments that this effect of the light (or whatever it was) lasted, she passed the police station and saw a car drive up with three men sitting in the back with a rug across their knees. All three got out, holding the rug bundled up between them, and she could see that the one in the middle was young, with a thin face, lank hair, and a blue shirt open at the neck, and that the other two, though wearing ordinary suits, were obviously policemen, whose solemn faces and awkward movements with the rug showed that the man between them was handcuffed and that they thought it proper to try to conceal this. All three seemed to be involved in a ritual which linked them by an interdependence far more solemn and inevitable than the handcuffs, as if their only concern was that they should play the parts assigned to them without faltering, and as if this concern, being common to them all, bound them together by affection rather than by steel.

In a few moments she had passed them and was round the corner, conscious of the weight of her shopping basket, and hurrying towards the car; but the visionary aspect of the little scene stayed in her mind and on the way home she tried, without success, to find a significance for it, because although she was an atheist she at the same time vaguely expected some kind of personal message from God which would upset all her beliefs and give her a special dispensation never to die.

Having missed Communion, Conrad had meant to go to Evensong, a service he liked and seldom went to, but now that there was to be an extra Cabinet meeting he would have to drive up to London instead, so he telephoned the Vicar to ask if he might read the Lessons at Matins rather than at Evensong and having obtained his agreement felt relieved from the obligation to go on with his writing, and decided instead that there was time to take Jess for a short walk before Church. In this way he could both avoid having to read the Sunday papers, which would be full of tiresome pre-judgements of the issues which were no doubt to be discussed at the Cabinet meeting, and make sure that he would be out if any of his colleagues were to telephone.

His political decisions had always been slow and solitary ones. He could also put forward quite a convincing case for politicians making as few decisions as possible, maintaining that this was the harder but wiser course, and that a politician's proper task was to react rather than to act and that in his reactions it was his feeling for events, for history, his instincts (based on experience) rather than his science, which should guide him. When he developed this theme, which he did sometimes when people came to lunch, his admirers were impressed by his wisdom and authority and by the humility with which he bore them, and more critical guests thought his theory too obviously applicable to his own career in politics, which was long and perhaps too free from controversy.

As he walked round the garden with Jess before Church, he filled his mind with thoughts of his immediate surroundings and of his plans for cutting down even further the maintenance involved, of having only grass to be cut and no beds to be dug, because of the scarcity and high cost of labour. Every now and then Jess, who was old, would stop and give a brief choking cough. Each time he watched her with concern and spoke to her gently before they walked on. The trouble was, her heart was going.

Back at the house, there was a message from the Home Secretary, asking him to telephone. He put it off until after Church, thinking that it would only be a question of discussing the Middle Eastern crisis before the Cabinet meeting—would he not join in making strong representations to the Prime Minister and the Foreign Secretary for more information, did he not agree that some of them had really been left disgracefully in the dark as to what the hell was going on? In fact he was wrong; the purpose of the Home Secretary's call was to tell him about his nephew's escape from prison.

Conrad enjoyed reading the Lessons. He had a good voice and such a loving familiarity with most of the Bible that he knew he read it well. This particular Sunday his enjoyment was marred by his catching sight of Daintry in the congregation. Five years ago, when they had first met, Conrad had been fascinated by Daintry: he now found him a bore, and knew that he would be unable to avoid talking to him after Church. Toad, he had come to call him, in reference not only to his vulgarity but to the fact that he now seemed to him to be a toady, or creep; and the great Georgian house which Daintry had resuscitated at immense expense Conrad amused himself by thinking of as Toad Hall. When Paul and his then wife Serena, Daintry's daughter, used to stay there and organise social activities which were supposed to amuse Daintry, Conrad used to allow himself a feast of sneering: he rather missed it after Paul's divorce. His connection with Daintry was not severed after Paul's quarrel because he was still a considerable shareholder in one of Daintry's companies, of which he had been a director until he became a Cabinet Minister when the Conservative Government took office in 1951. He retained a certain admiration for Daintry as a business man, if only for the immensity of his operations.

In spite of his equivocal attitude towards Daintry as a neighbour, as the saviour of a worthwhile piece of local architecture, as the lessee of his, Conrad's, pheasant shooting, Conrad had no hesitation in giving him his due as a brilliant financier and a very rich man—two facts which Conrad fully recognised as giving him a great deal of power. It was only in superficial ways that he disapproved of Daintry: fundamentally he had not much against him, as long as he did not have to speak to him after Church.

It was, however, as he had foreseen, inevitable.

'A word in your ear, old chap,' said Daintry, taking his arm in a confidential way and walking with him along the path which led only to the door through the wall into Mount Sorrel garden. Conrad dragged his steps, hoping to avoid having to ask him in for a glass of sherry.

'Bang on, that sermon, I thought, didn't you?' said Daintry, whose nostalgia for his happy times in wartime Coastal Command was still only too often reflected in his speech. 'We're lucky to have a chap like that. Hard cheese about his legs. Look here, about this Canal business—have you a minute or two?'

'I'm a bit tied up this morning as a matter of fact. I've got someone coming to see me before lunch.'

'Valves,' said Daintry.

'I'm sorry—?'

'If the Canal is closed there'll have to be a pipeline. Daintry Automation must supply the valves. No need to look at me like that. I know you. Might as well ask Her Majesty the Queen for prior info. I'm only thinking ahead. If it comes to that point we want to make sure it's an English firm that gets that order. It will be an international effort of some sort. We'll put in a competitive tender and we want full Government co-operation.'

'You certainly are thinking ahead.'

'Why not? Things can move fast, you know.'

'You're talking about a possibility which is highly problematical.'

'Telling me. I'm perfectly in favour of giving Nasser a bashing for his cheek but on the other hand it's not a bit of good without American support, and you'll never get that with Ike so near a Presidential election. That being so, if the Gyppos have first got to learn to run the Canal, then as like as not have a war with the Israelis, I see no reason why the Canal might not be closed for years—and why the world's shipping might not manage perfectly well without it. Just so long as there's a nice pipeline for the oil.'

'I think most people would find that a pretty unpalatable solution.'

'That's as may be. There's a lot of unpalatable things around these days especially for the poor old English who won the War. That's life, isn't it?' said Daintry, sounding as if it suited him well enough in spite of everything.

'Of course if the time comes I'll talk to the President of the Board of Trade. You should write to him too. You know him, don't you? But not yet.'

'Yes, I know him. But he needs to be nagged. Short on guts I find him. He ought to be out there selling us. That's the patriotic thing to do these days. Well, I'll say cheerio if you've got something on. Don't want to butt in.'

He turned back just as they reached the door in the wall, saying loudly over Conrad's faint polite protest, 'Look in any time you're over my way. I'm always there at weekends. Give you a glass of champagne any time you like. You can see the latest tricks this decorator fellow's been up to. You wouldn't believe it. Paint mixed by the Adam Brothers' own fair hands—must be, to look at the bill—see you.'

He strode vigorously away, huge in his new winter tweeds. Conrad opened the garden door, on which the white paint was chipped where the sun had blistered it and

greened along its lower edge by rising damp from the flag-
stones beneath, and walked through, smiling slightly.

'He's no fool,' he said aloud, giving the door a push to
make sure it was properly shut behind him. 'You may not
like him,' and here he was talking in imagination—as he
rarely did in fact—to his son Henry. 'But he's by no
means a fool.'

Agatha had once said in her annoying way that she admired Daintry for not having become any less awful with
success, but Conrad knew that Henry would have preferred East Stainton to have become a ruin rather than be
inhabited by Daintry. 'There's no point in houses that size
these days, anyway,' he had said.

Conrad now saw very little of Henry and believed himself to have accepted without bitterness the fact of having
a ne'er-do-well son; nevertheless in the course of his
musings, which often, probably because he lived alone,
took the form of imaginary dialogues, usually half silent
and half muttered aloud, he sometimes entered into long
explanations and justifications with his son; a fact whose
significance never occurred to him.

'You can't just write off a man like that,' he muttered.
(Henry, rather than listening, was digging Dora's grave.)
'He's shrewd, backs his judgement, gets things done. You
have to have people like that.'

The telephone was ringing again as he approached the
house.

Henry was cooking the lunch and Agatha was talking.
He had given her a large glass of rather unpleasant Cyprus
sherry and told her that she was to sit by the fire and read
the papers, but she had said she did not want to be alone
and had followed him into the kitchen, where she now sat
on the table, unwisely warming her sherry by clasping the
glass in both hands, slightly swilling the contents about

inside it as if she were tasting a rare burgundy. She had begun to talk in the rather excitable and exaggerated way in which she sometimes expressed herself to Henry and which left her the option of pretending she had not meant a word of it should he begin to look disapproving.

'First of all we have to liberate ourselves—by thinking a lot—from illusion and insincerity,' she said in a lecturing tone of voice. 'In other words from deception about outer reality and deception about inner reality. And then, you see, what we have to do is, we have to link ourselves to the history of our species.'

'Must we?'

'Yes, because you have to have movement. You can't resist movement. It's all the universe is, all our history is. Flow, and flux and things. Love allows flow, non-love dams it.'

'It certainly does,' said Henry, who meant to imply that therefore she was not to stop loving him in spite of any grounds she might think she had for doing so.

'But love doesn't allow—mustn't allow, or it will go wrong—mustn't allow for the proper play, in action, of our individuality. So we have to have work. And everything else is absolutely irrelevant. Love and work. It's all there is.'

'What about art?' said Henry. 'Move, will you.' He opened a drawer and began to take out knives and forks.

'The less it's thought about the better,' said Agatha, shifting sideways along the table. 'If there's love and work there'll be art. Loving and working you're bound to dream, and your dreams will be myths about your deepest pre-occupations worked out in dream language, and that is art.'

'Good Lord,' said Henry. 'And I don't even have dreams.'

'Oh you do, only you forget them. If you don't dream

34

you die. They've proved it, with experiments.'

'I hope this hasn't got anything to do with politics,' said Henry.

'Well, that's only a question of organisation, isn't it? Giving theories names and getting emotional about them is all a great bore. Whatever system makes it possible for the most people to love and work with the greatest freedom of choice and the least feeling of injustice must be the best, that's all. There are probably several different systems that are equally not bad, several that are equally terrible. But it's no use thinking any government is going to be worth supporting whole-heartedly—it's like being a prefect at school—I mean one's on the other side of things.'

'I expect you're right,' said Henry. 'You always are.'

'Oh no.' Agatha looked upset. 'I've been talking too much.'

Henry came over to the table and put his arms round her. She leant her head on his chest and said, 'I wish you loved me.'

'I do.'

'I thought I was going to be married and live happily ever after. It's only because it isn't like that that I had to start all this thinking.'

'It is like that,' said Henry. 'You must believe me. You must.'

'Yes.'

'You must trust me. You believe in taking risks. You must trust me. I love you.' He squeezed her so hard that she began to cough.

'Can't we go to bed?' he said.

But the children were coming in, cold.

Agatha took their coats off.

'The baddies were on a train and I shot them,' said Lucy.

Agatha picked her up and sat on the table again with Lucy on her knee.

'Once upon a time—'

'Mn?' said Lucy.

'There was a little girl who lived in the middle of a wood with her mother and father and her elder brother and one day her mother was so hungry—'

'No, she didn't.'

'That she cut her up in little pieces and put her on a plate and poured gravy all over her and ate her up.'

'So then,' said Lucy, nodding several times, 'the little girl jumped herself together again, picked up the gravy, poured it all over the mother, wrapped her in brown paper and put her in the dustbin.'

'She didn't really, did she?' said George, whose nature was such that he found it very hard not to believe what people said even when he knew they were speaking of impossibilities.

'Of course not, silly. Come on. Lunch. Your father has cooked lunch for you.'

'Did Daddy really cook it?'

They were impressed, ready to believe that because he had cooked it it must be exceptional. He fussed about, covering up with activity the thought that he might be in danger of accounting to Agatha for his selfishness by presenting it to her in the sort of light in which it could be expected to appeal to her. Looking at their faces, Agatha's pale and tired and therefore touching, the children's beautifully healthy and expectant, he felt very fond of them all.

Part of the bargain which Agatha had struck with Paul's deliverers was that they should bring him immediately to the assignation in the woods. She had attached great importance to seeing him once before he went into an exile which she supposed would last for ever. For reasons of their own the men had chosen Swindon as the place in which he was to be concealed until they took him out of the country, and it was there that they drove after leaving Agatha.

About the middle of the morning Paul was put down in a crowded shopping street. Following the directions he had been given, he walked steadily for some distance, took several turnings and came into a quiet street of small houses which looked so respectable that he wondered at first whether he had memorised the directions correctly, but since it was important not to linger or look around or in any way attract attention he walked on at the same even pace, past little garden gates of slatted wood, squares of grass and minute flower-beds in which roses were still blooming, and front doors with an oval of frosted glass at face level. One or two of the front doors had faded canvas curtains in front of them, such as he remembered seeing in his childhood on the doors of seaside boarding houses. Whether their purpose was to protect the paint on the door from the effects of the sun or to provide privacy and shade when the door was left open in the summer he had never known, but he remembered the smell and feel and faded look of one such in the doorway of the boarding house in the Isle of Wight to which he had been taken every summer until the war, first by his mother and father and then, after his father's death, by his mother and Orlando, who was later the father of Agatha and perhaps of Imogen, and who was at that time in his heyday. Pain gripped him in the stomach and would have stopped him had he not known he must not stop—'Oh poor thing, poor thing,' went through his head, meaning, Poor Paul, poor me.

Without hesitating he pushed open the low gate of number 39, went up to the door and rang the bell. The door opened at once and he went in. It was shut behind him and a quiet figure moved past him in the dim hall, said 'Upstairs', and led the way. He followed and was taken into a small back bedroom painted pink with a brown dado and containing little but a double bed covered with a slippery brown bedspread.

'Here,' said the woman.

She was small and fiftyish, wearing a green nylon overall and bedroom slippers. The expression on her face was quite clearly one of distaste but he thought he could see a subdued excitement too.

She jerked her head towards the door.

'He's coming with the clothes.'

She was not interested in him. The excitement, if it was there, would be for the money. He wondered how much of Agatha's money she was getting.

'You haven't such a thing as a cup of tea, I suppose?' he asked, smiling.

She went out without speaking and shut the door. Almost immediately she returned with a bundle of clothes.

'He says to change,' she said, putting the clothes on the bed.

She went out again without looking at him. She was going to be hard to charm. He would try though. His mother had been able to charm anyone. He looked into the mirror which hung over the mantelpiece, but after one brief gaze into his own eyes he moved away and began quickly to change his clothes. The suit they had given him was the right size, though nasty: certainly they were efficient.

The woman came in, put a mug of tea down on the bedside table—'How kind,' he murmured—and took away his own clothes. He hoped they would remember their promise to let him have them back on the boat. It was a better suit than anything he would be able to get where he was going.

He heard the stairs creak and then a door was quietly shut. That would be the man who was wearing his clothes, distinctive duffle coat and all, and who was to leave the house and walk back along the street for the benefit of any inquisitive neighbours, so that if necessary he could be passed off as—what, he wondered?—the man from the hire purchase perhaps.

Paul drank the tea, which was tepid and for which he had only asked in an attempt to strike up some sort of relationship with its provider. He tried to fight down his depression and fear by telling himself that the plan was working, that the most difficult part was already over and that there could be no doubt that Charlie Edwards, who had put him on to this organisation, was right: they were highly efficient and worth the expense. He congratulated himself for his foresight in having approached Charlie the moment he knew that his arrest was imminent. He was going to get away with it. He was going to be all right.

Later the woman brought him two cold sausages, some bread and cheese with pickle and another mug of tepid tea. She also brought the paperbacks for which he had asked the men in the car, but she still refused to be drawn into conversation. He foresaw that the three days in this little room might be a kind of Purgatory. He asked the woman for paper and a pencil and began a long letter of justification to Agatha.

Henry worked for a firm of insurance brokers in the City, a job which bored him and for which he was paid £8 a week. He had no qualifications, since he had failed to pass any exams at Oxford, but it had been vaguely hinted to him at the time when his forthcoming marriage to Agatha had forced him to look for a job that there might be 'prospects' in this one. They had not yet materialised, and since Conrad thought it right not to let Henry have any of the money which he would have at Conrad's death until such time as he had shown himself capable of looking after it, his financial situation was bad. Agatha had a small income of her own from the money which her father had left in trust for her, and it was on this that they mainly lived, while Henry's salary went almost entirely towards the paying off of the mortgage on their house, the deposit on which had been released by Agatha's trustees.

They had a blue Ford Thames van, on the hire purchase. The visibility from the driver's seat was not good, or at least not good enough for Henry, who was a driver who could use a lot of visibility, but to have had windows cut in the back part, which would have improved matters in that way, would have meant that it was liable to tax as a private vehicle rather than as a commercial one, as which in its present state it was able to pass.

When he had driven Agatha and the children back to London on Sunday evening, and had helped Agatha to give them some food and put them to bed, Henry said, 'I might go round to the pub for a bit, to see if there's anything on television about Hungary.'

'Do, yes. I'll go to bed, I think,' said Agatha.

He went out hurriedly so as not to see the expression on her face, and drove off in the van, over-revving the engine.

When he had Agatha and the children in the car he drove with a modicum of circumspection, but alone he reverted to his pre-marital road habits, which were undesirable. So, turning out into the King's Road, he did not wait for a pause in the stream of Sunday night returning traffic, but accelerating noisily lurched out into the middle of it, passed a couple of cars on the wrong side of the road so as to avoid the avenging fury of the Jaguar he had caused to brake uncomfortably hard, and was then forced back to his own side by an oncoming van, whose furious hooting mingled with that of the car in front of which he was obliged to squeeze. He then unexpectedly shot across the road again (not having had time to get the right-hand indicator mended), down Smith Street, where he narrowly avoided a minor television personality and his psychiatrist wife who were crossing the road rather slowly after a meal at the Indian restaurant, screamed round the corner into St Leonard's Terrace and drew up in front of the house where Sally had a flat: his expression throughout the drive had been abstracted but serene and he had been whistling the tune of a calypso of which the first words were 'Brown skin girl, stay home and mind babee'. He would have been irritated if their possible application to his own case had struck him, but if it had been that which had influenced his choice it had certainly been unconsciously, because the few minutes of the drive had been a break in conscious thought, which seemed to return to him only as he pressed the bell and felt the happy disquiet which the immediate prospect of seeing Sally always induced.

She was wearing a black dress, drawn in rather tightly round her knees and without much back, so that her own beautiful one was exposed, high-heeled black shoes and a tiny sequinned hat with a green feather in it.

'How lovely you look,' he said when they had reached her flat, which was at the top of the house.

'You don't really like it, do you?' she said, turning to look at him, posing slightly with her hand on her hip.

He felt indeed on looking at her such a sharp sense of disappointment that he could hardly speak. He thought she looked ridiculous.

'I think it's lovely,' he said. 'Very smart. Can I give myself a drink?'

'Of course. I'm meant to be going out to dinner.'

'Oh.'

'With Johnny Marner.'

'Oh.'

'He rang up to say he was just back from America and would I have a little quiet supper at the Aperitif—can you believe it?' She picked up the telephone, and dialled, took off her hat and shook out her golden hair. 'My *mother*—would you believe it?—and so *ill*, I'll have to put her straight to bed, this awful spring 'flu—my dear, it's so much *worse* when you get it in the autumn—that's the whole point—and to drive up from the country, can you believe anything so silly?—oh I must, she's so *old* and so helpless—tomorrow would be lovely—'bye—he's mad about me.' This last seemed to Henry to have been said, quite loudly, before the receiver had been replaced, and therefore probably to have been overheard by the handsome middle-aged peripatetic political peer who had been so lightly dismissed. He began to feel better.

'Do you know what he told me when he rang up before? Just like that on the telephone—they are so indiscreet, those sort of people.' She went through into her bedroom, still talking. 'He said that the French and the English are definitely going to declare war on the Egyptians any minute and that they're banking on the Russians being so worried about Hungary that they won't butt in. Don't you think it's quite extraordinary to tell me that? It's going to be short and sharp, over in a minute, he said. It's all been planned down to the last detail. Don't you think it's rather exciting?'

'I suppose it's only his opinion,' said Henry. 'I mean, surely only a very few people know a thing like that for certain?'

'He sounded awfully sure about it,' said Sally, coming back into the room wearing a white cotton dressing-gown. 'It seemed a good idea, I thought. I'm sick of England being pushed around, aren't you? I mean, people seem to forget who we are, don't they?'

She looked serious as she said this, standing in the middle of the room, transformed into such ravishing beauty as a few minutes ago might have seemed too much to hope for, and gazing at him earnestly.

'Who are we?' said Henry foolishly, full of delight. He kissed her gently on the temple, gave her her drink and said, 'Tell me about your weekend.'

'My dear,' she said, settling down in a comfortable chair. All the chairs in her flat were comfortable; it was warm and well lit and had pleasant colours on the walls and Indian rugs on the floors; it was also usually very tidy and clean, for Sally was an efficient girl and in respect of housework would have made an excellent wife, as she quite often pointed out. 'My *dear*, I didn't know such people existed. Quite close to you too, I'm amazed you don't know them.'

'Gloucestershire is a world apart.'

'Well, anyway there they all were. So many of them too. We went from house to house and each was richer and grander than the last. And so big and so handsome—the people I mean, the women as well as the men—and I've never had so many passes made at me in two days, all the men and most of the women. It must be something to do with horses, all that *straddling* must be suggestive. Anyway they were terribly kind to me. You wouldn't have liked them though.'

'Did you?'

'Well, I suppose they're a bit square, really. But you know me. I like anywhere where there's money and lovely things and people are nice to me. It's my deprived childhood or something.'

'And will you be seeing much of him do you suppose?'

'I suppose so. Although really I ought to find someone who's not impossible, oughtn't I? I mean I'm getting old. I'm twenty-four.' Actually she was twenty-five.

'I don't think so. I don't say that out of self-interest, though you might think I do. It's quite hard work being married, for the wife I mean.'

'Not for the husband?'

43

'All the advantages are on the husband's side.'

'Well, I could marry someone very rich. I mean, I can't go on messing about for ever. Soon I'll be wrinkled and horrible and no one will want to take photographs of me and I'll starve.'

'I'll support you in your old age. I'll be richer then. I'll buy you a little house in Maida Vale and come round once a week with a bag of gold.'

She sighed. 'How many times have I told you I'm not that sort of woman,' she said. 'What am I going to do with you, Henry?'

'You're going to jump into my arms,' he said, putting down his glass and holding them out to her.

Agatha had inherited from Orlando a cluster of half-ruined buildings on a remote hillside in Tuscany, where he had spent the last years of his life. She always hoped that one day she and Henry would be able to spend more time there, and had resisted Conrad's argument that the most sensible thing to do with the place was to sell it; but for the time being they had let the house where Orlando had lived for a small rent to an English couple who both worked for an international organisation in Rome. They used it for weekends (without taking much care of it), and the land was farmed by the peasant family who lived in the only other fully habitable house. For the last two years Agatha and Henry and the children had spent their fortnight's holiday camping in the tower house which Orlando had been in the process of restoring at the time of his death.

Agatha never dreamt about the tower house, but the other one, the one where Orlando had lived, appeared frequently in her dreams, usually empty, sometimes with a wind blowing through it and banging the doors, sometimes as the scene of a search in which she hurried from room to room and failed to find what she sought; and

44

though the dreams were invariably worrying ones, they left behind them a feeling which was in a way satisfying, a feeling that they were in some sense true.

It was from one of these dreams that she woke to the realisation that the alarm had failed to go off and that Henry was going to be late for work. Unless she hurried, George would also be late for school, which was worse, because George hated being late for school.

She woke them all, and hurried to make the breakfast. George and Lucy were eating their cereals when Henry came into the kitchen. Agatha saw from the expression on his face that he was uneasy about having come back so late the night before. She turned away from him sharply, suddenly angry, and poured out some coffee for him. He took it from her and put an arm round her shoulder. She moved away quickly, took away the children's empty bowls, and began to dish out their scrambled eggs. Henry made a sound indicative of reproach.

'We're late,' said Agatha, not looking at him.

'I was only trying to be friendly,' said Henry.

'If you have to try, it seems hardly worth it,' said Agatha.

Henry drank his coffee and left.

She ran after him up the stairs and stopped him by the front door.

'I don't mind your being late,' she said. 'I'm used to that. I mind your coming in with a stupid self-conscious face when all that matters is getting George to school on time. You're so frivolous. What does it matter? What do we matter? What right have we to personal happiness? It's quite irrelevant.'

Henry looked at his watch.

Agatha turned and ran upstairs into the lavatory. She heard the front door shut and clutching her stomach as if in physical pain sank to the floor in a crouching position, her head bent onto her knees. After a few moments she stood up, washed her face, stared into the mirror saying, 'God forgive me' and then ran downstairs into the kitchen saying, 'Oh, God forgive me. Jesus Christ forgive me for my manifold sins and wickednesses.'

'Why have you got wet knees?' asked Lucy.

They had finished their breakfast but were still sitting there banging their plates with their forks, co-operating in a complicated rhythm.

'George, why haven't you put your coat on? Quick, we're going to be late.'

'I didn't know,' said George, getting off his chair and looking anxious.

Agatha looked down at her knees and saw that her stockings had in fact been soaked, even in those few moments, by her tears. She smiled, as people will who have cut a finger and feel a certain wonder and pride at the amount of blood they have shed.

'I must have knelt on something. Come on, hurry.'

The school was only three streets away. They ran most of the way. The little yard at the side of the building was empty.

'They've gone in,' said George.

'It's only just after nine,' said Agatha.

'It's all right,' said George. 'It doesn't matter.'

But it did, to him. She could see that it did from his anxious face as he ran in, unbuttoning his coat as he went. She was supposed to love him but could not get out of bed five minutes earlier to spare him this distress.

She could have grasped the railings and shrieked until the fabric of the universe was torn asunder, but said to Lucy, 'We'll buy the lunch on the way home.'

Imogen, late, ran flustered along a passage, to be stopped at the end by a shout from the girl at the reception

46

desk.

'Hey, wait, your uncle rang up. He wants you to have dinner with him tonight.'

Imogen stopped, gasped, clapped her hand over her mouth.

'What's the matter?' said the receptionist.

'Did he say why?' asked Imogen, still looking aghast.

'No. He just said to go to the usual place at eight o'clock.'

'Oh. Well, I can't, but I'll ring him up. Thanks.'

She walked on more slowly. The morning papers had reported Paul's escape from prison and described the search which was taking place for him. Imogen had not been in touch with Agatha, preferring to know nothing about any of it. Surely Conrad could not possibly know that Agatha had been involved? But she, Imogen, knew nothing, must know nothing. She tried to tell herself that Conrad could have no reason to suppose otherwise. It must be money again, she told herself, she must have been spending too much money again.

Familiarity had taken the terror out of that particular situation, and her spirits began to recover. That was what it must be. She would go and have a drink with him before dinner and say she was sorry and it would be all right. She knew that Conrad had always had a kindness for her in spite of the many aspects of her character which he might be expected to find reprehensible: she was much better at dealing with him than Agatha had ever been.

Conrad's first thought on hearing of the escape had been that Agatha might have been involved, and all that worrying day he had at the back of his mind a confused picture of walls, ropes, Paul and Agatha; remnants of the dreams which had seemed to fill the night; Agatha climbing, dressed in black as she had been at Orlando's funeral,

47

Agatha swinging on the end of a rope, banging against a high windowless wall, Agatha on a ladder, himself following, Agatha reaching up to clasp the bars of a prison window and kicking the ladder away behind her so that he fell and, falling, looked down an immeasurable distance to the ground outside the prison building, where under a small thorn tree lay a form curled up in the position of an embryo, and whatever it was, this form, it was he, Conrad, who had let it fall.

The day was a worrying one because it was the first on which he really took in the fact that the international situation, which of course he had known for some time to be serious, was suddenly developing at an uncomfortable pace, that he was not quite certain what the Government of which he was a member was doing about it, and that whatever it was he was not sure that they were going to be able to do it successfully. He was not himself immediately connected either with Foreign Affairs or with Defence, and it appeared that those who were, together with the Prime Minister, had either been moving very fast or, as was beginning to seem more probable, very secretly, into a position where an ultimatum was now to be delivered jointly with France to the Egyptians and the Israelis, the foreseeable result being that the Israelis would accept the terms and the Egyptians refuse them, whereupon there should be a 'short and sharp' attack upon Egypt. Conrad spent the day trying to find out how short and how sharp this attack could be expected to be.

He had not been ignorant of the general thinking of his colleagues about the Egyptian crisis and he was not out of sympathy with it. He would have supported aggressive action against Nasser at the time of the nationalisation of the Suez Canal in July. His doubts now—apart from general speculations about the uses or misuses of Cabinet government—were only as to timing and planning.

'It's got to work' was his theme throughout the day. 'We're going to be in very bad trouble if it doesn't.'

He found one or two equally troubled sympathisers but on the whole it was not a popular approach. He felt aggrieved that his reasonable caution should be taken as faint-heartedness; even more aggrieved that his views, which had been freely expressed over the last month or so, should have been so obviously discounted. He was used to the committee system and knew that when decisions were made, particularly ones requiring immediate action, there were always a few members who for one reason or another had their doubts disregarded and were swept along in the current which an action begun soon generates: he was not used to being among their number himself. A brief interview with the highest authority that could be found to spare the time for him that morning resulted only in display of bad temper and an implication that his own record did not give him the right to criticise. He had resigned from the Chamberlain Government, but not until after Munich, and he was therefore tainted with 'appeasement', a word which still aroused strong emotion and which in his case warred with his reputation for wisdom and high-mindedness.

'It's not the same,' he said doggedly. 'Nasser is not Hitler.'

'I understood we had your support. The service chiefs are absolutely confident.'

'I can't help still being worried about America. You don't think there ought to be one more personal telephone call to Ike?'

'We've considered all these things very carefully. We must be allowed to get on with the job.'

Of course he pledged his support. Anything else at this late stage would have been a personal disloyalty which was not to be considered. He thought that the policy was probably the right one, as long as it succeeded; only he had many years of experience on the periphery of the innermost circle of government and the feel of the thing at that moment was not quite right.

The evening papers carried news of the intensification of the search for Paul. He read them in his flat, having walked back there from the House of Lords to meet Imogen. She was late. He thought about Agatha again. All her life she had been a worry to him. If only his wife had lived, Alexandra, fleet of foot like the goddess Diana, whom animals had but to see to love—and pain began to rise in him as it rarely did now, and the thought of its rareness made him say aloud, 'They think I don't suffer— they don't know—they don't know how lonely I am.' He began to walk up and down in his dull little room. 'I must be tired.' He poured himself out a whisky and soda. 'Difficult times. Difficult times. God help us. Help us, O Lord.' And at once he began to feel calm, and there floated into his mind what God meant to him, which was the stone walls of the church at Mount Sorrel, and the grass on the graves of his forebears, and his deep though ritualised relationship with the men who worked in his woods, and his father gently introducing to him the idea of duty, which seemed one of the most beautiful ideas in the world, and the love of God and the fellowship of men, and wanting the village to be able to be proud of one.

'One does one's best after all,' he said, gazing out of the window at the back of St James's Park Underground station. 'One does one's best.' He took a gulp of his whisky and soda, and looked at his watch, but without too much impatience. Imogen was always late.

When she arrived she was breathless but pretty.

'That's a very fetching garment you've got on,' he said, giving her a kiss on the cheek. 'Have a drink. What would you like? I'm sorry you couldn't dine with me tonight.'

'Yes, I'm going out, I'm sorry.'

'Where do you young people go these days? The Four Hundred? Quags?'

'You might get taken to the Four Hundred, yes, but it's awfully boring. You probably just go to small restaurants —you know, the Matelot or the Ox on the Roof or something. There's a place called the Green Room where everyone I know seems to go a lot—it's a club—underneath Ciro's.'

'Oh Ciro's, yes, I know that. Ah well, I expect you'll get a much better dinner than I can offer you at the House of Lords. I've got to be there this evening. There's rather a lot on.'

'No, I love going there. It's so peaceful and fuddy-duddy. I feel really safe. I even like the food being bad.'

He laughed. 'I feel like that myself sometimes. But unpleasant facts penetrate even there now and then. I say, what an awful business this is about Paul, isn't it?'

'Awful,' said Imogen feelingly.

'As if we hadn't all suffered enough.'

'That's exactly what I said,' said Imogen. 'I mean, to myself, when I read the paper.' She blushed slightly.

'Have you talked to Agatha about it at all?'

'No, I haven't.'

'You didn't ring her up or anything? I'd have thought you might have.'

'Yes, well, yes I might have. But I didn't somehow.'

'Was that because you thought she might be too sympathetic towards Paul?'

'I suppose so. Yes, I suppose it was.'

'She wouldn't do anything foolish, would she?'

'What sort of thing?' asked Imogen, blushing again.

'Sheltering him from the police, for instance.'

'Oh no. No, I'm sure she wouldn't do that. It would be much too dangerous for one thing. I mean, I suppose they're watching us probably.'

'You don't think she knew anything about it, do you?'

'No.' Imogen shook her head vigorously. 'No.'

'Why are you so sure about it?'

'Well, I—because—well, I mean it would be so silly—'

'Agatha sometimes is silly, with the best of intentions as often as not. She never mentioned to you any plans for getting him out? Even a long time ago, when he was first arrested? After all he must have known he was going to be convicted.'

'It would have been something he'd arranged himself,' said Imogen. 'Before he went to prison. I mean, he had a lot of criminal friends.'

'Who?'

'Oh I don't know. One says that sort of thing. I haven't the faintest idea really.'

'You must have been thinking of someone.'

'Well, I suppose there was that man Charlie Edwards, you know, who used to be a burglar and wrote a book about it. He'd have known all those sort of people.'

'Yes,' said Conrad thoughtfully. 'So you don't think Agatha had any sort of foreknowledge? I must say, that's a tremendous relief to me.'

'I'm sure that if she did it would only be in some quite unimportant way. I mean, obviously Agatha couldn't have worked out a complicated plot involving keeping him hidden and getting him out of the country and all that sort of thing by herself, could she?' She looked at him appealingly.

'My dear,' he said solemnly, 'make no mistake about it. Anybody who knew anything at all and has not told the police is committing a crime. We may wish that Paul hadn't been sent to prison, even more than we wish he hadn't committed the crime which led to it, but the fact remains that it is the law of the land, and that is just about the most important thing there is. Without the rule of law, the whole of our society would fall apart. We have to hope, you and I, that Paul will be recaptured. We have to hope he will serve his sentence. Because that is the law.'

'Oh I do. I do hope that, I really do. I know that you never really got on with Paul, but I did. We had some nice times together, and when he wasn't drunk or being hurtful for some reason, he could be so nice, Paul, he really could. But I know it's no good trying to escape, I mean if you've broken the law there it is.'

'You'll tell me then if you hear anything or think of anything that could help the police?'

'Yes, I will, of course I will,' said Imogen earnestly.

'Don't worry about it too much. The police are a highly competent body of men. It will probably all be over in a day or two.'

'I hope so.'

'Poor Paul, what a fool he was.'

'Yes.'

'I mustn't keep you. What time's your date?'

Imogen looked at her watch.

'Oh gosh, I'm late!'

Conrad laughed. 'He must be used to it by this time, whoever he is. But I'm sorry it was my fault this time. I've been rather bothered about all this. You've set my mind at rest. Now don't you start worrying, will you? We're all in it together after all, aren't we?'

'Yes. Oh yes, of course we are.' She had gathered scarf and bag and stood restlessly running the former through her hands. 'Thank you so much for the drink. It was super. I must run.'

She kissed him and was gone before he could say he was going too. He hesitated for a moment, wondering whether to telephone the police about Charles Edwards. Then he decided that they were bound to have got on to him already, and that anyway he would be needed in the House of Lords; so he followed Imogen, more slowly, down the dark passage outside his flat, waited a few moments for the ancient creaking lift, was hauled down in it by the melancholy lady in what appeared to be Salvation Army uniform who manned its rope control, and walked out into the rather cold autumn evening to see almost immediately in a telephone-box near the entrance to the Underground the distinctive blue colour of Imogen's pretty dress. He did not pause, able without doing so to satisfy himself as he passed that it was indeed Imogen.

If she had wanted to telephone her friend to say she was going to be late, she could easily have done so from the flat. It seemed more likely that she was telephoning Agatha, to warn her of his suspicions.

All this pain will wear my flesh away, thought Agatha. I'll be all bone, beautiful white bone, blown clean by the wind. Then my pride will have had its fall. Isn't it pride which makes me suffer so? Because someone knows—in some charming room, a delightful girl—that my husband doesn't love me. He says he does but it isn't possible because he also says he loves her—whom I have seen with shining hair across a room. I saw her before he did. I saw her lean forward sitting at a table, slightly hunched, turning to her neighbour '—but you're so *good* at—'. Just that I heard, and saw her dazzled smile and the curve of her cheek and chin and felt a shock of recognition almost indistinguishable from desire, so closely was I, am I, physically involved with him; sometimes my flesh forgets that we are separate. Well, she has a look of Caroline, that's all, who was his girl-friend before me.

If it were all pride I could subdue it. I can dig out pride, jealousy, fear, all maggots in my wound, and still it bleeds.

I could cry for ever.

And at other times would shout love, for this I was born to do. I love you and you and you, and you dead and you living, and you heroes and you traitors. Only so can movement move, and love be clothed with flesh. And so can figures neither one thing nor the other be turned to gold.

'The only escape, the only way open to me, was to become everything of which Uncle Conrad disapproved,' wrote Paul. 'In that at least you must admit I have been successful.'

It was cold in the little bedroom. He had asked for some form of heating and the woman had brought a single-bar electric fire. He sat in front of it, with a blanket wrapped round his legs, writing on his knee. He had already covered fourteen sides of the cheap lined writing paper she had brought for him.

There was now a rather unpleasant smell of singeing in the room because he had sat too close to the fire and the blanket had a small brown patch where it had begun to burn. It was getting towards the end of the afternoon, the sort of time when the woman might be expected to bring him a cup of tea. Having moved away from the fire a little, he tried to concentrate on what he was writing but could not help listening for the quiet, slightly shuffling footsteps which would mean she was on her way and would find him out, would sniff, probably, and say, 'You've burnt the blanket.' He would offer to pay. Trapped there with her horrible blanket round his legs, looking up into her horrible unyielding face, he would fumble for money in the pockets of his alien cheap suit.

'If only I had a long-suffering temperament, like you,' he wrote to Agatha. 'You don't know how lucky you are.'

The tone of his letter had so far been detached and even ironical but under the pressure of the persecution to which he now felt that the whole situation of the burnt blanket exposed him, it began to change.

'It's always been the same. Is it my fault that I was the one to inherit our mother's temperament? I know you were only seven when she died and can't have much idea of what she was really like, but she was "hypersensitive", as Conrad once scornfully put it, long before she went round the bend. Even when she was married to my father there were terrible scenes sometimes. She minded everything so much. Some people do. And think of being like that—a minder—and having to take what I had to take. A neurotic mother, a pompous ass of a father—oh how he grovelled before the system of which he was really a victim, thinking himself a proper little capitalist and never daring to admit what a pathetic slave they'd made of him. Some fool of a psychiatrist before the trial tried to make me say I wanted revenge on my father. I didn't. I wanted revenge *for* him. For the fact that they'd turned him into a stupid little creeping snob. They tried it on Orlando too, and damned nearly succeeded, but in the end he was too intelligent for them and got away. Got right away, you see. That's what I could never do. I always stayed hanging around on the edges, looking through windows, watching other people having a nicer time than me. Oh the cold feeling of that glass that was always between me and them.'

When he had written the last sentence he felt enormously cheered. He read through the whole passage again.

'Excellent!' he said when he had finished it. 'Really excellent.' He laughed aloud, thinking how pleased Agatha would be. Hadn't she said she wanted him to write something? He'd always been interested in that sort of thing. There'd been that time at school when he'd had that really marvellous idea for a film. If only the whole scheme hadn't had to be dropped because of the way he'd been organising the money-raising, it would have been really good—and incidentally annoyed a lot of people—and then he could have gone on in films and everything would have been different.

But it was not necessarily too late. A sort of picaresque semi-fictionalised autiobiography was what he foresaw. And what a film that would make. After the success of the book of course.

The shuffling footsteps had approached without his being aware of them.

She held out the mug of greenish-looking liquid and said, 'Tea.'

'Oh!' He took it, and as she turned away, evidently preferring to overlook the smell of singeing rather than enter into any kind of conversation, he added, 'You're too sweet, you really are.'

Perhaps she was deaf.

It was quite clearly understood between Agatha and Henry that Henry disapproved of introspection and thought that Agatha did too much of it. It was also understood between them that up to a certain point he admired her for it, although there was no question of his taking up that sort of thing himself.

This convention allowed Henry to avoid admitting to himself the extent of the unhappiness which his relationship with Sally was causing Agatha. It seemed to him that neither of them should think about it too much. The bad time had been when he had realised that his emotional involvement with Sally had become too deep to be concealed from Agatha. He had talked to her about it, and had been surprised and sorry to find that while she did already know about the relationship, this knowledge had been able to co-exist with a belief that it simply could not be true: her imagination had been unable to grasp the reality of a situation which the evidence made obvious. Their conversations at that time had inevitably been long and painful and he believed that they were at one in thinking that that had been enough of that. He had agreed with her that their marriage could not stand his being seriously in love with Sally and that the proper thing for him to do was to withdraw, wind the thing down, change it from a love affair into a sentimental friendship. Agatha had said that she could stand a sentimental friendship.

So, driving home after work through the rush-hour traffic, he felt only a minor disquiet in case Agatha should be in a bad mood when he got back, but was otherwise confident, and resolved to be very nice to her as soon as he saw her so as to make it quite clear that on his side all was love and amiability. His optimism was superficial, as perhaps it always must be in one whose determination to live for the moment is the result of a conscious decision. Under it loomed or slowly swirled doubts to which he refused to give a name, great gloomy sea things beneath the thin ice on which he skated. Wasn't he behaving well? Of course he was. At the same time, was it really allowable to spin out the vaunted withdrawal from the impossible situation quite so long, enjoying meanwhile the best of both worlds?

It was better not to think about it, to sing, or drive dangerously, or spend too long a lunch hour with some friend from the old days trapped like him in a boring job for the sake of subsistence. Because to take advantage of two such sweet girls would certainly be wrong: but the softness of thinking of them in that way had an element of self-congratulation in it, and also in the case of Agatha an element almost of daring, because to call Agatha a sweet girl was not an adequate description.

Part of Henry's charm for women was that in his easy way he had a very quick appreciation of the intricacies of personality. It was a gift which entered into his relationships with men too—and these were the ones which he himself thought of as proper friendships; nevertheless more than one pretty girl had annoyed a jealous admirer by saying, 'He's such a *friend*—you couldn't possibly understand.'

This subtle sympathy meant that without ever having given her character much sustained or detached consideration he had a clear understanding of Agatha's mode of being, which was very different from his own. There was a certain element in it to which he was drawn and by which he was frightened, and which he considered quite inappropriate in relation to anything in his own life or the lives of most people he knew, and that was that she tried to be good. He saw her doing it, and often by her own standards failing, and sometimes it annoyed him on her own behalf because it made her life so much less comfortable than it might have been, and sometimes it made him want to hurt her.

The last reaction was presumably an envious one, because it came to him at times when, returning to her from some mundane activity, or even from being with Sally, he would find her doing something not in itself important, cooking perhaps or playing with the children, or if they were in the country lying on the grass or gardening, and know at once from her calm welcoming smile that she was happy, but with a happiness whose calm was rapt, whose fullness was ecstatic, a happiness which had nothing to do with him, and to which he felt that ordinary people, who lived in the world as it was and did not bother themselves with abstractions or tiresome moralities, had no hope of aspiring. At these times he occasionally said something unkind to her, for which he was afterwards sorry.

This evening when he came back from work he immediately recognised another typical situation. His long lunch had made him later than usual in leaving the office and by the time he got home the children were already in bed. The narrow hallway of the little house was dim and rather cold. Agatha was sitting halfway up the stairs, crouched over the book she was reading and which she was having to hold close to her eyes because of the lack of light. She looked up when he came in, and blinked in a distant sort of way as if she had been concentrating very hard on what she had been reading.

Henry turned on the light, said, 'You don't look very comfortable.' She stood up, jumped down the last of the stairs, kissed him on the cheek and led the way into the sitting-room, where a fire was burning and the curtains were drawn. Having turned on the lights at the door, she went over to the lamp behind the sofa and switched that on too.

'That's better,' said Henry.

She would prepare the room for him but never sit in it herself until he was there: something in her character seemed to prevent her from ever making herself comfortable. She would be cold but not put on another jersey, hungry but not eat anything except a crust of bread unless there was someone with her, tired but not go to bed, sad but not distract herself with idle pleasures; he found that maddening.

Knowing his feelings, she said, 'I was so comfortable on the stairs.'

He frowned.

'Luxury,' she said. 'I was in a bed of luxury.'

'You know I don't like that sort of thing.' But he smiled as he sat down. 'Is Joe coming to supper, did you say?'

After Joe had left, Agatha told Henry that she had helped Paul to escape from prison.

Joe Hertz had been a friend of Henry's at Oxford and had become an equally close friend of Agatha's. At the beginning of their marriage he had been the third who by his appreciation showed up their happiness, a role he played with a slightly wistful and never malicious self-mockery, for which they were both grateful to him; some of the times all three had spent together had been among their happiest. As well as that he was Henry's friend, with a shared past and a shared sense of satire, and Agatha's friend, with a shared tenderness of heart. It was typical of him that he should feel comfortable as an adjunct to their marriage, because his place seemed always to be a peripheral one; touching the circles of love and gain, ambition and self-abnegation, heterosexuality and homosexuality, still more or less uncommitted. From Oxford he had gone into advertising, as many clever people with a slight literary bent were doing at that time. A series of atrocious puns made him one of the highest paid copy-writers in his firm. He liked the money and despised the work. In the same way he enjoyed the company of privileged and amusing people, a number of whom had become his friends at Oxford, and despised himself for spending so much time with them. He felt he had not only an obligation but perhaps a vocation to help others less fortunate, or even to make a more far-reaching contribution towards the improvement of society. Anyone seeing him among the usual group of friends at a party might have been forgiven for not guessing it, but he was not at all sure that he might not be a new Karl Marx. He was always giving himself another month, two months, six months, and then he was going to Leeds to be a school-teacher. Leeds, ignorant of its destiny, was luckily unconcerned by the delay.

Since he was quite honest about all this ambivalence, it gave him a certain ironical way of looking at things which, while it revealed his own discontent, nevertheless made him a very sympathetic companion. Evenings spent with Joe were without tension; and it was easy to go on talking after he had left.

'I've done something rather wrong which I have to tell you about,' said Agatha.

The thought popped up in his mind as if it had been rung up with a *ting* on a cash register, 'If she's been unfaithful she's *out*. I don't want to hear anything about it, she just *goes*.'

'I wish you wouldn't frown so,' said Agatha.

'What is it?' he said through his teeth.

'I helped Paul to escape from prison.'

'Oh.' Relief spread gently through his muscles, easing him more comfortably into his chair. 'How?'

'Some people came to see me asking for money and I gave it to them.'

'Who were they?'

'Professionals of some sort. I think he must have arranged the whole thing before he went to prison. I didn't ask too much about it but you know how he always did know quite a lot of criminals. They told me they could do it all if I gave them seven hundred pounds. They promised it would work, so I did.'

'How did you get the money?'

'Sold my shares. And then I met them with him in the woods the other morning—the time Dora got run over.'

'She wasn't with you?'

'Oh no, no. I hadn't seen her since the night before, when we lost her. So I saw him and he seemed all right and they were going to hide him somewhere and then get him out of the country when the search had died down a bit.'

'Good Lord. I hope it's all right.'

'The thing is, I could go to prison, and I've been rather worried about that because of the children.'

'And me,' he said quickly.

'And you. Do you think it was wrong to run the risk? He hadn't anyone else to help him, you see, and he is my brother.'

'Surely you couldn't be sent to prison for that?'

'Yes, I could. It could be two years. Some things are taken awfully seriously by the law. Look what a heavy sentence they gave Paul. Treachery's very badly thought of, so's helping people to avoid the law. I did think about it quite carefully first. I'd get remission, I suppose. And then I know you do care for the children very much. I think the Dutch girl could probably move in permanently —it's a success, that, the children really like her—and I thought I could write them a letter every single day which they could read at breakfast and if there aren't posts every day from prison I could give you a whole lot at once which you could give them one at a time. Perhaps, at weekends and things, Sally would help sometimes, I mean going on expeditions with them and that sort of thing?'

Henry did not answer, so Agatha went on, 'It would be rather difficult to explain to George because he's so very law-abiding but I think if I put it quite simply he'd be able to understand. I have worried rather about school but I think five-year-olds are too young to be interested, don't you?'

'Yes, I should think so,' said Henry, but she could see that he was not thinking about George. He had not liked her mentioning Sally. She wondered why. They looked at each other in silence. How easily, he thought, she refers to Sally, assumes I should be with her; does it mean she doesn't care? Agatha thought, He never goes for essentials; what does it matter if he doesn't like my implying that Sally might do something useful for a change, when what we're talking about is the children and how to protect them from suffering if their mother goes to prison?

Henry thought, We can't stare at each other in silence for ever, and sensing something of her feelings he stood up and said rather formally, 'I think you were quite right. I'll

63

support you, of course, in any way I can.'

Conrad walked up and down in the Central Lobby of the House of Commons waiting for Henry. There was a good deal of activity. The afternoon's sitting had not started and there were a number of Members of Parliament hurrying to and fro looking preoccupied, and some others meeting constituents for whom they had found seats in the public galleries: outside there was a queue of the less fortunate: the Prime Minister was expected to make an announcement later in the day. Conrad paced up and down slowly. Some of the Members greeted him, and hesitated as if they would have liked to talk, but though he was polite he was not encouraging and they passed on, respecting what they felt must be his legitimate preoccupations. He was not happy. His morning's meetings had not been satisfactory. He was tired. He was trying consciously to suspend his thoughts, with the result that his head felt like a nest of cotton-wool in which a few phrases lay supine—'heavy-hearted', 'deeply unhappy', 'ah, there you are. Let's go through to the other place and have some coffee', which last lay there in preparation for Henry's arrival, already overdue. He was coming from the City, could not spare the time for lunch apparently, but would come immediately afterwards, by Underground, which was why Conrad was where he was, arousing mild speculation as to which Member he might be waiting for and what it had to do with the crisis; because today there was certainly a feeling that something was going to happen. The Israeli attack on Egypt was filling the newspapers and the House of Commons was expecting to be told that afternoon what the Government was doing about it.

Just as Conrad muttered, 'He's late' he saw Henry, and was struck by how young he looked, walking up the steps among much older people, handsome, suit too tight and hair too long, they all want to look like Teddy Boys these days. 'Ah there you are. Let's go through to the other place and have some coffee.' He put his hand on Henry's shoulder as if to pilot him through the groups of people standing about; he smiled at the same time, as if he had just said, 'Yes, I'd love to see the Art Room, old chap' on the school speech day. Deftly manoeuvring a passing secretary into a collision, Henry managed to throw off the hand.

'I'm sorry I couldn't manage lunch,' he said.

'Never mind. I expect you're very busy. As a matter of fact we've got quite a lot on here too at the moment.'

'Have you?' said Henry. 'What? Cyprus or something again?'

'The Middle East more.'

'Oh.'

Conrad thought, The young don't read the newspapers, they don't read anything, they go to the cinema.

'I saw an excellent film last night by the way,' he said. 'You really must see it when you get a chance. I got dragged along to this royal command thing, you know, for some official reason. I usually hate that sort of thing but I really enjoyed it. *The Battle of the River Plate*. Perfectly splendid. They hardly embroidered it at all. Awfully well acted.'

'Who was in it?'

'Oh, Quayle I think the fellow's called, and Gregson the other one. Quite convincing. It was a splendid thing of course for the English. The great German battleship, the *Graf Spee* with her eleven-inch guns, outfought by the three little cruisers, *Exeter*, *Ajax* and *Achilles*. Beautiful. Do try and see it.'

'Yes, I will, mn.'

'Come along then, sit down, it's a bit quieter in here. Just some coffee please for two. Well now, how are you? I haven't seen you for a long time. How's Agatha? And the

65

children?'

'Very well, thank you.'

'And how's the job going?'

'Not too bad. Rather boring.'

'It's a grind at first, I daresay.'

'Yes.'

'Good news about Hungary, isn't it? It really looks as if they've got what they wanted. Not that you can trust the Russians of course but it looks as if they're prepared to give them a go.'

'Yes, it is good.'

'No apathy among the young there anyway. Wonderful how those students seem to have organised themselves. Students, poets, writers, the traditional idea of the revolutionary. Romantic, don't you think?'

'Yes.'

'Now the one among your friends I really do like is that young Jewish boy, Hertz. How is he getting on?'

'All right, I think.'

'Still in advertising?'

'Yes.' For some reason, Henry felt reluctant to tell his father that Joe had said the other night that he was about to set off for Austria with a group of people taking medical supplies to the Hungarians. Anyway perhaps if the revolution was over he would not be going after all now.

'Sugar? Oh no, of course you don't, do you? I ought not to, I suppose; getting fat.' He wasn't. 'Still, what does it matter at my age? I daresay I've only a few more years to run anyway.'

Henry gave him a quick knowing look, refusing to rise, and Conrad laughed, suddenly feeling more cheerful.

'Look here, though,' he said. 'Give me a sign some time. You know what I mean. I could make things much easier for you and Agatha if only I felt the time had come. It would be a tremendous help to me if you could take on some of the responsibilities of Mount Sorrel. It's not that I don't want to hand over, but if only you could take a little interest, or at least show some signs of getting on in the world a bit, the job and so on, you know what I mean.'

Henry nodded, even smiled, but when he raised his eyes for a moment they looked to Conrad wild and far-seeing as an eagle's and like an eagle's full of a remote uncomprehending scorn.

'Well anyway,' said Conrad quickly, 'we must talk about all that another time. I know you've got to get back. The point is, about the wretched Paul. Have the police been to see you yet?'

'No.'

'They will. And what I want to say to you is this. For God's sake if there's anything you know, anything you can think of that could possibly help them, tell them. I know Agatha was Paul's only friend—in the family anyway—and of course I admire her loyalty to him, but Agatha's a person of very strong feelings, as I don't need to tell you, and I dread to think that they might lead her into doing something foolish, like being less than frank with the police or even giving shelter to Paul if he should turn up. That would be disastrous. She's got her children to think of. I do hope she realises that.'

'I'm sure she hasn't the faintest idea where Paul is.'

'The police know about her special relationship with Paul. If she doesn't co-operate with them she'll be in very severe trouble indeed.'

'He'd be mad if he came to us. He must be miles away by now.'

'This man Charles Edwards. He was a friend of Paul's, wasn't he?'

'He certainly knew him, but I never heard that they saw a great deal of each other. I don't know much about Paul's life during the last few years. He really never cared for me particularly. Agatha and he used to have lunch together from time to time but I'd really hardly seen him for a couple of years before all this.'

'He'd behaved so badly over all that Daintry episode. I don't think any of us should have been seeing him really. However, there you are. Tell her what I've said, will you?'

'Yes, I will. I'll tell her as soon as I get home this evening. And thank you very much for the warning.'

Conrad pushed back his chair. 'I must get on with the various unpleasant tasks I have to do this afternoon. And you must get back to yours, no doubt.'

'Yes, I must.'

They stood up.

'Don't bother,' said Henry. 'I'll find my way out.'

'I'll walk with you.'

As they walked along the dark passage, Conrad thought almost guiltily of Henry's use of the word 'warning'. Had it been a warning? Had he meant to say, 'The police are on their way; get your story straight?'

That morning he had telephoned the Inspector in charge of the case to tell him to get on to Charles Edwards, and had mentioned in passing that if any of the family knew anything it would be Agatha. He had had to do that after seeing Imogen in the telephone-box. He had meant his message to Agatha to amount to an order, that she was to co-operate with the police and not be silly. But if they chose to interpret it as a warning, did it matter? After all he did not want them to suffer. He wanted them to stay out of trouble.

'We've all got to be sensible about this thing,' he said.

'Yes, of course,' said Henry.

They had come to the arch of King Henry's tower.

'Go back in, it's freezing,' said Henry. 'I'll tell her, don't worry. See you soon.'

'Goodbye,' said Conrad, pausing on the top step.

68

Henry looked back from the pavement, raised a hand, thought briefly, Christ, he looks a million, and after walking a little way towards the Underground station began to run, because he was cold and relieved to get away and incidentally late back at the office. His hair lifted from his forehead by the cold wind, he put on speed, beginning for some reason to smile, and dashed past the now slowly moving queue outside St Stephen's entrance. Some of the people in the queue, trapped in their slow progression, looked at him curiously as he sped by with his smile in the opposite direction.

Conrad had waited at the top of the steps in spite of the cold, and had seen him start to run. It had worried him. Why should he run, except for some suspicious reason?

'People I hate,' wrote Paul: 'Uncle Conrad, Cousin Henry (your husband), all schoolmasters, judges, policemen and taxi-drivers (taxi-drivers are Fascists, don't ask me why but you will never meet a taxi-driver who is not either an overt or a crypto Fascist: at the time of my trial every taxi-driver in London wanted me hanged). People who have done me injury: my dead brother Stephen, my dead father Leonard, my dead mother Judith, Uncle Conrad, Cousin Henry, all schoolmasters, judges, policemen and taxi-drivers. People you might think I would hate but I don't: Daintry, his daughter Serena (my ex-wife), my dead step-father Orlando (your father). People I like: You. Although you are extremely nasty to me. If ever we talk about my problems you are thoroughly stern and bossy. And yet, when we talk, you talk to *me*. With you I am free, you don't force me into a role conceived by you and for you, to suit your own purposes. That is what all the others do. To do that to another human being, what disrespect that shows. Amounting a gross evil. Only the really smug would dare. But English and smug are synonymous words. Perhaps it was because he was brought up in France that Orlando wasn't so bad. There was a time when I did hate him (oh yes, I have been quite liberal with my hate) and that was when I was finally expelled from Eton and he made me go and work in some foul office in Leicester. Then he wasn't nice, and I was just the tiresome step-son, in trouble again. The war got me out of that. Though the Army was worse of course. But after the war I got to like him again. He'd become free, like he was at the beginning, he wasn't blinkered by phoney frames (in the American sense, spectacles, though hardly in his case rose-tinted, and in the sense too of a correct gold frame edging a picture, and of a frame of mind, a frame of reference, a framework on which to balance all those sacred institutions by which the Conrads order their worlds, frame upon frame—a cold frame too, if you like, to grow a frightful warty cucumber in, and amounting altogether in the end to nothing more nor less than a rotten frame-up).

'Where was I? Oh yes, among people I hate. So much of my life has been spent among people I hate, at home, at school, in the Army, in the office. At the trial my defence made out that I'd sold those papers just for the money, but it wasn't true. I was selling much more than a few drawings, and the money only interested me in the sense that it was the handful of silver with which the traitor is rewarded, and I wanted to feel like a traitor.

'There's quite a certain secret joy in that feeling which you might find hard to imagine. The invisible worm that flies in the night, that's me. That's what I was up to when I left Logan Holdings, the family firm after all. I knew I could get Daintry to take it over and push out Stephen and put me in to run it instead. I married Serena to consolidate my position with Daintry, thus betraying not only her but myself as well because I don't like going to bed with girls. As to that, the funny thing is, I managed quite well at first while I disliked her, but as I got fond of her it began to disgust me—so she thought I didn't love her just at the time that I almost did. I'd never been fond of anyone before, not in that rather protective, potentially domestic way, and of course she didn't understand, couldn't wait, thought she'd better run off with that fatuous playboy Hayford while she had the chance. Otherwise we just might have made it. She used to cry sometimes when she'd had some setback, like not being asked to a party (she took her social climbing so terribly seriously I couldn't help being touched) and I used to comfort her and stroke her hair and tell her that never mind, one day Raine Legge would ask her to be on the committee for the Save the Idiot Infants Ball, and at those moments I almost loved her. Perhaps it was because she was the only person in the world I could help, because I knew more smart people than she did. I did a lot for her in that way and she's very good about that, she never forgets to be grateful. After all she'd never have met bonny Bunny Hayford but for me, let alone all those shiny magazines and things I fixed for her. No, she's all right in her way, Serena. She came to see me in prison, and you know how terrified she was of bad publicity. It really meant something, her doing that. Do you know what she told me then that she'd never told me before? I didn't go to the divorce hearing, as you know, but her lawyers were worried because there wasn't much of a case against me, she was the one who'd left and it looked a bit tricky, so they told her all she need do was write one sentence on a piece of paper and pass it to the judge and it would go through without a murmur. She did and it did. She'd written, 'My husband is a practising homosexual.' The funny thing was, at that time and for her sake I wasn't practising. I was quite out of practice, in fact. It took me *hours* to get back into the swing of it. No, but seriously, talk about loaded dice.

'I digress. Not that I'm short of time. Time's wingéd chariot is pinioned for me. But not for you perhaps, with your little ones and your dreadful dog and your handsome husband, those four domestic tyrants. So we will leave the digression, which was marriage—oh God, will you read this far?'

Would she? He pushed away the blanket from his knees, put down his pad of paper and his pencil on the chair, stretched himself, and walked to the window. The net curtains smelt of soot. Opposite was a blank wall of purplish brick. Looking out of the window afforded no relief.

'Lonely,' he said, his forehead against the window pane. 'It's very lonely here.'

He turned back into the room and gathered up the scattered sheets of paper which he had already covered with writing and had thrown behind him onto the thin brown satin bedspread. When he had collected them together he banged them gently on the top of the chest of drawers to bring them into line and was agreeably surprised to see what a fat sheaf of manuscript they made. Of course it was worth doing. Of course Agatha would read it. He had better get on with it so as to have it finished by the time they came to collect him for the next stage of the journey.

He sat down again, wrapping the blanket round his legs. This way the time would pass—ridiculous sad waste of time—what was that? T. S. Eliot or something—time before and time after—because of course he always had been really a literary person and no one, not one single schoolmaster, not his mother who was too self-absorbed to care, not his father who wanted him to play cricket and be manly, no one had ever encouraged him to be himself, or bothered to try to guess what sort of self himself might be.

Except Agatha.

'I'll try to send you some sort of address,' he wrote, 'when I get there, if I ever do. Here in this horrible little room it's sometimes impossible to believe I'll ever get out. It's worse than prison, the confinement being more solitary, it feels like a very bad punishment indeed. What if they never come back for me?

'But I'll go on. About Stephen. You were very kind to me at the time of Stephen's death, and you were with me a lot, in spite of all the other things you had to do. I don't know if I ever thanked you for that. You once said to me when Imogen was having one of her crises—didn't she have a brief disastrous brush with Bunny Hayford before he got involved with Serena, or am I imagining that? anyway, her heart was broken and she was in floods of tears for three days—you said—sadly, because you wanted to do more—"You can never do anything for people in trouble except lend them your presence," and it's true but people are often quite reluctant to do that, they'd rather pay for something or send flowers. But you're good at it. "Wait a minute and I'll give you my full attention" is what you say when you're busy, and then you do. You are generous with your full attention. I'm not becoming maudlin. In many ways you are quite tiresome as well.

'Anyway, at that time you were very considerate of my feelings, but you had in fact misjudged them. I didn't mind very much when Stephen died. People thought I'd as good as killed him. Perhaps I had, but there was so little to kill. Most of him had been dead for years. He had no real existence of his own, Stephen. From the very beginning he changed his opinions to match those of the most powerful person in the room. When we were children he always agreed with Nanny—he used to sit beside her cutting out pictures of the Little Princesses as good as gold, till he was about fifteen as far as I remember. He was just a sackful of

73

pretentious clichés—and lurking inside it all somewhere was a little vicious undeveloped embryo of what might have been a human being. All that that was capable of feeling was fear, an overwhelming paralysing fear. That part, the only part of him that was almost alive, must have been glad to die.

'Of course I didn't mean him to kill himself. I suppose I overdid it, I got excited, the feeling of power went to my head. I could have eased him out more delicately. I hadn't really expected Daintry to give me the Managing Director-ship straight away and tell me to make a clean sweep. It seemed almost too good to be true. Perhaps I felt it couldn't last, and that's why I was in such a hurry. I really had them all hopping, though. And the games I was play-ing with the share price at the same time—I made a couple of hundred thousand in a week, you know. What I didn't give to Serena I lost later. Serena loved money. No, I should have stuck with all that, I should never have quarrelled with Daintry. I had a good thing going there. The only bad thing was Stephen killing himself. He could have got another job. He'd lost face, that's all, and quite a lot of money, I suppose. But how could I know he'd go home to his frightful house in Godalming and kiss his frightful wife and his appalling fat child and go upstairs and shoot himself in the mouth?'

'Stupid ass,' shouted Paul suddenly, jumping up from his chair. He staggered slightly because the blanket was wrapped so tightly round his legs. He freed himself and began to walk up and down in the minute space between the window and the chair.

'Stupid bloody fool,' he shouted.

Everything had suddenly gone terribly wrong. Furiously, he kicked the chair, which fell over. He bent to pick it up, then stopped, listening. There was silence. With luck the woman was out. She seemed to go out most afternoons, where to he had no idea. He picked up the chair and sat down on it to read the pages he had just written. Agatha would not like them. He would have to re-write them. What a bore. He felt exhausted already. Was it because Agatha would not like that part that he would have to re-write it, or was it because it was not quite true? It was so hard to know. He sat slackly in the chair, thinking formlessly of Agatha, Stephen, what had happened then, what was happening now.

He went towards the bed, to lie down, and as he reached it suddenly collapsed onto it, and clasping the slippery brown bedspread with both hands pressed it against his face. A feeling of appalling loss overcame him. There was nothing to cling to except the horrible bedspread, everything else had swirled away into limitless dizzying empty space, in which he was suspended, nameless and abandoned, in enormous agony of mind. Raising his head from the bedspread, he saw the wet stains of his tears and began to sob, to bellow really, like a child, pressing the crumpled bedspread onto his face to try to muffle the sound. He knew all this. He had had it before. It was the worst pain in the world.

Every weekday afternoon Agatha went to work in a bookshop in the King's Road and Willy, the Dutch girl who lived two doors away, came to look after the children. It was a small bookshop and had been started many years ago by Miss Auriol Bannister and Miss Felicity Wickham, both of whom were still at the helm, or rather Miss Bannister was at the helm and Miss Wickham was a slightly desperate first mate.

Their association had begun in the thirties when they had both been involved in some kind of movement or other—quite what it had been Agatha had never made out, except that it had involved high principles of a left-wing variety, walking tours, pamphlets, free love and fun. They both looked back on that time with nostalgia, which extended to the early days of the bookshop and the wonderful kindness and camaraderie of certain great names at the mention of which Miss Bannister's and Miss Wickham's eyes shone with uncritical love and loyalty. Some afternoons these titans of an earlier age would be recalled over a cup of tea in the chaotic little back office, while Agatha listened and the customers pocketed the books in the shop at their leisure, or finding no one to buy them from, settled down to read them on the spot. Dylan, the most marvellous talker in the world, Augustus John, the wonderful man, evenings in pubs, the beauty of one, the wit of another, the self-destructive fury of a third, all heroes of a glorious lost Bohemia, free, quite often drunk, always inspired with the true poetic frenzy—only 'Bloomsbury we never cared for'. Agatha loved it when they talked like that. The trouble was (from the business point of view) they could find nothing in the current literary scene to command a similar allegiance. More and more often Agatha found herself on her afternoons urging Miss Bannister to do her shopping or to take a publisher's representative into the back office for a thorough scolding, and Miss Wickham to have another go at the accounts, which were years behind, or—and here she had been surprisingly successful—to slip off quietly to the cinema. In their absence she was usually able to sell a few books. If they were there it was harder.

'Grossly over-praised,' Miss Bannister would trumpet from the back of the shop as an innocent customer handed something to Agatha to be wrapped. 'Not a novel at all, mere reportage—I'd wait for the paperback.'

'Not nearly as good as the film,' Miss Wickham would murmur as a customer picked up a book. Confidence undermined, he might put it down and turn to another. 'Auriol says the publisher ought to be ashamed of himself.'

That was another thing. Publishers from time to time incurred Miss Bannister's displeasure: this meant that for a period, usually quite brief, no new book from that publisher was allowed into the shop and those already in stock were so denigrated by Miss Bannister as to deter all but the boldest would-be purchaser.

'We don't stock books from Macmillan,' enquirers would be told, as if the whole of that large and reputable organisation had suddenly swung into the purveying of filth, and only an immediate conciliatory visit from the Sales Director (for Miss Bannister had her own little reputation) would make her relent.

Agatha had not liked Miss Bannister when she first went to work in the shop because it had seemed to her that Miss Bannister bullied Miss Wickham. When she got to know them better she understood that their relationship had been going through a bad period. Miss Wickham had just acquired what was in effect a wig, although she herself called it a hairpiece. Her own hair, which was very fair and wispy, had been becoming increasingly thin on top, and the scalp which showed through drew attention to itself by a curious shininess, so that the wig might be said to be an improvement, for all that it was so unmistakeably a wig. Miss Bannister however thought it a mistake, and said so. All this was just at the time that Agatha was starting to work for them, and Miss Bannister's mockery was not restrained in front of her. To escape it, Agatha's first afternoon, Miss Wickham, her long gentle features easily assuming the expression of a scapegoat going out into the wilderness heavy with the sins of her people, silently took up her macintosh and crept towards the door.

'Going to see what you can pick up at the Doorway then?' said Miss Bannister with pretended jollity from behind a pile of books.

The Doorway was a Lesbian club just round the corner.

Neither Miss Bannister nor Miss Wickham, despite speculation among some of their clientele, had ever been
Lesbians.

Miss Wickham seemed to sink several inches closer to
the ground, murmured, 'Must get something for supper,'
and, opening the door a very little, squeezed out. Agatha
wondered how soon she could decently give in her notice.

She was forestalled by Miss Wickham who a few days
later, sitting upright on a hard little chair in the shop,
occupied with her embroidery (she was extraordinarily
skilful, and always at her most calm and philosophical
when she was doing what she called 'my work'), said of
Miss Bannister, 'She's tremendously kind, you know.'

Miss Bannister was in the back office with the representative of a firm of religious publishers, whom she had
invited in for a glass of port. 'She'll even take some of his
books, I expect, though she loathes religion. His wife died,
poor man, quite unexpectedly, of a cerebral haemorrhage.
She was only forty. They had no children, which makes it
worse, I think, don't you?'

Agatha, dusting shelves, agreed and said, 'So she's not
always so fierce?'

'Oh no,' said Miss Wickham, shocked. After a minute
she went on in a confidential sort of way, 'I suppose you
think she's been a bit caustic about my hairpiece, but the
trouble is, you see, she thinks I'm making a fool of myself.'
Her long deft fingers moved without pause.

'Isn't that rather interfering of her?' said Agatha.

'Well, but one does interfere when one's known someone a long time. Besides, she thinks it's all to do with some
new friends of mine, which it is really. They're awfully
nice people. They live in the flat below me in Rosetti
Mansions. He's retired from the Colonial Service, and
she's so good-looking—it was her idea about the hairpiece.
Auriol can't bear them. She thinks they're Philistine and

right-wing, which they are of course. And, you see, that really means a lot to Auriol. As a matter of fact,' and here she lowered her voice, 'I joined the League of Empire Loyalists.'

'Good heavens!'

Miss Wickham nodded. 'Glenda—that's the wife—is terribly keen. She even travelled all the way to Glasgow to interrupt Eden and got thrown out of the meeting. That was when Auriol found out about her because it was in the papers. Auriol was so upset that I resigned without ever telling her I'd joined. I realised how much she would have minded if she'd known. Politics have always meant more to Auriol than to me. So I was only a member for four days. You won't tell her, will you?'

'Of course not. Weren't they rather annoyed?'

'Glenda was cross, yes, but not for long. The League was very stuffy about it. I got quite a nasty letter and they only returned half my subscription.' Miss Wickham suddenly gave a sort of explosive giggle and bent down over her embroidery exposing the clear line where the hairpiece failed to blend into the soft grey curls at the nape of her neck.

All this somehow combined with the glimpses of chaos she caught when trying to help Miss Wickham with the accounts to make Agatha feel that to ask for a rise in pay, as Imogen had recommended, was out of the question: besides, three pounds a week was better than nothing.

Following her revolutionary policy of trying actually to sell some of their stock, Agatha moved quite rapidly when the man in the overcoat approached Miss Wickham, holding out a copy of Colin Wilson's *The Outsider*. Miss Wickham peered at him doubtfully, without taking the book.

'Rather French—' she said hesitantly.

'Frightfully slapdash,' said Miss Bannister, in passing.

Agatha, having by now approached the customer, took the book.

'I thought it was very good,' she said firmly, and carried it off to the other side of the shop in order to wrap it up.

The man followed her, watching. 'What time do you finish here?' he asked quietly.

Agatha looked at him, and was immediately reminded of the two men who had been with Paul when she had met him in the woods.

'We close at half-past five,' she said calmly.

'I'll walk home with you if I may,' he said without expression. 'I'd like to have a word with you.'

She looked at him coldly, as if she had no idea what he was talking about.

'It's about your brother.'

She merely looked a little thoughtful, then said, 'I come out just after half-past but I'm usually in rather a hurry because I have to put my children to bed.'

'I won't keep you,' he said. He picked up the parcel and his change and left. Agatha sat down for a moment. She felt certain he must be a blackmailer. She tried to reassure herself: she could have given nothing away, so immediately had his appearance put her on her guard, and besides, her strength must be that she knew so little. But supposing he knew something—Paul's present whereabouts, for instance —and wanted money not to disclose it to the police? She had no more money. As the afternoon went on, she began to feel sick.

That morning she had had one of her failures, a lapse from grace. She had woken up too early, had found her head full of unwelcome thoughts and had lain there at their mercy, hearing the sound of milk-bottles and Lucy's mad morning singing. Henry had been out late again the night before and of course it wasn't fair; if you had a wife who loved you without reserve but also without, she really did believe, any of the diseases which made love non-love, if you had a wife like that and said you loved her, you didn't love another person on the same level. It made no sense, and she was merely weak in suffering it in silence. It was just an awful injury he was doing her. How could she respect him now? How could he fail to realise to what an extent he was using up her goodwill? The feeling of righteous indignation was perhaps to be preferred to the other feeling, the feeling of pure pain. On the other hand it made her so angry that she suddenly sat up in bed and pummelled his sleeping form as hard as she could with both fists.

He did not move but made a faint groan.

'You've used up all my love,' she said furiously. 'You think it's inexhaustible but it isn't. I haven't any left.'

He turned slowly towards her, hunching himself deeper into the bedclothes. Pulling his pillow down towards him, he shut his eyes, apparently settling himself for more sleep.

'Henry!' she shouted.

He opened one eye apprehensively. She immediately thought, What a horrible woman I am.

'You look awful,' she said more mildly.

He turned onto his back, moving cautiously, and opened and shut his mouth two or three times as if experimentally.

'I can imagine more cheery awakenings,' he said.

'Does Sally get angry with you?'

'Yes.'

She was silent, thinking of Sally, whose feet would be like the feet of girls at school, long, bony and bare, in the enforced intimacy of the changing-room, legs thin-skinned tending to be blue before netball, numinous soft bosom exposed for a moment in the struggle with a shirt. She had known a girl rather like Sally at school, Clare somebody, who had had the same mouth turned down at the corners and wide-apart eyes, and would be now an object of desire, like Sally, an object of love, like Sally. What else could one expect?

The hated concept of herself as millstone reappeared.

'You must have what you must have,' she said dreamily.

But then they had made love, and more emotion had been required of her, and he had said ferociously—and he had never said it before—'You must forgive me,' and she had been shocked, because she did not really want to consider it in that light. She had said, feeling that it referred to much more than just the present situation, 'I forgive you, past and now and to come I forgive you.'

Because of course it was perfectly clear what she should do, or rather, as was often the case and often much harder, not do; and of course she blamed herself, hated herself in fact, when she failed: the trouble was that it was exhausting, and that she sometimes doubted her ability to sustain it. There would be nobody to forgive *her*.

It was all still on her mind when she left the shop—it was always on her mind, that was one of the aspects of the situation which she found impossible to control—so that her fear that her connection with Paul's escape might be discovered had to co-exist with that, as well as with her anxiety to get back to the children as soon as possible in case Willy, who liked to leave punctually at six, should disconcert them by showing her impatience to be gone (which in fact she never did); and so when the man in the overcoat stepped out from the doorway of the dry-cleaners she hardly paused, merely saying, 'Do you mind if we walk straight home?'

'Not at all. There were just one or two questions. I didn't want to bother you at home.' He held out a card in a leather holder.

When she saw it she did stop, but only for a moment, to look at him in unbelief, and then she went on walking.

'You could easily have come to see me at home,' she

said freezingly. 'My children aren't afraid of policemen.'

She was furious that his surreptitious approach should have frightened her. She thought that policemen should be kindly people in uniform who told you the way to places and helped you find somewhere to park your car.

'I thought at this stage it might be better,' he said in a firm but detached tone of voice which did not put her at her ease. 'Have you any news of your brother?'

'No.'

'He hasn't been in touch with you at all?'

'No.'

'Would you expect him to get in touch with you?'

'No.'

'Why not?'

'I expect he's left the country.'

'Why do you say that?'

'Don't people usually, when they escape from prison?'

'Not necessarily, no.'

They walked along the pavement of a quiet road, rather fast because Agatha was setting the pace.

'You've no idea where he might have gone to?'

'No, I haven't.'

'Can you think of any friends or associates who might have been involved in this thing?'

'No.'

'We understand that you were on friendly terms with your brother.'

'Yes, I was.'

'And yet you can't think of anything that might help us in our enquiries, no questionable associates, nothing you remember him saying at any time, after the trial for instance, when you went to see him?'

'No, I can't,' said Agatha in a tone of voice which implied only too clearly that he would be the last person she would tell if she could.

83

The man was silent for a few moments, keeping pace easily with Agatha. Did he have rubber soles? She seemed to hear only her own footsteps, sharp and cross on the pavement.

'We rather understood,' he said in that tone of voice, soft, indifferent and deadly, which was so much more appropriate for the criminal she had at first thought him, 'from your uncle, that you would be disposed to help us.'

She knew she was in danger, but he had made her angry, so much so that her upper lip was slightly trembling, and the fact that she could not control the trembling made her more angry.

'How can I help you when I don't know anything?' she said. 'Besides, I'm afraid I find your approach very putting off. I don't see why you couldn't come and see me in the ordinary way, without having to be so secretive about it.'

He held out another piece of paper, this time with a telephone number written on it.

'If you think of anything ring this number,' he said. 'Ask for Inspector Skarrett.'

She took the paper and he turned away, walking at the same steady pace down a side-street, past a pub.

She felt she had been childish.

'It's all power,' wrote Paul, 'that's all any of us are after. From the first moment we're born we can't wait to get on to that ladder, and start grappling our way up, and kicking off the people on the lower rungs. Some of us are straightforward about it, like Daintry, and some of us (women, for instance) are more devious, but disguise it how we may it's the only basic driving force we have. And before you start saying it's wicked remember it's the only thing that differentiates us from animals.

'I remember Orlando quoting some French saying about "in order to be happy it is necessary that the others shouldn't be" and being rather annoyed because my mother agreed with him—he thought it wasn't a suitable thought for her, only for him. You don't remember him then of course, but he had a lot of charm in those early days, when he was aggressive and ambitious and rather a show-off. Rather a shit too. No, we don't like people because they're nice, whatever you may say.

'Anyway, that's all I ever wanted, just my share of the feeling that the others hadn't got what I had. And I've always had the opposite feeling. Even you have never understood how much I've felt on the outside. If I'd been inside I should have been a different person—because one is conditioned by one's social circumstances. All right, to some my social circumstances might have looked good, but I was too near to people with better. I was on the fringes of the Establishment, but not in it. That's even worse than being right outside. I was conditioned into being a spy, an underminer.

'Oh, Agatha, you are a good girl to have put this writing business into my head. I've so many ideas now I don't know when I'm going to get them down on paper. Because that's another one, isn't it? "The Role of the Spy in the Modern World"—a *really* highbrow article, full of references to Sartre and Colin Wilson and so on. Do you suppose I can become an Overseas Member of the London Library when I'm in my South American exile? Will you make a few preliminary enquiries? I shall send it to *Encounter*. Then you'll be proud of me, won't you?

'Anyway, that's how I see myself, as a destroyer, and it's up to someone else to do the rebuilding.

'You may ask why I didn't start destroying sooner and why I spent so long in the silken tents of my enemy. Good question. Answer (1) I was always destroying in my heart, with my scorn. (2) Lack of opportunity.

'I did really have a horrible time in the Daintry organisation after Stephen's death, although it may have looked from the outside as if I were getting everything I wanted. Daintry despised me. He probably always had, ever since I asked him for a job. He must have seen through me then and known what I was after. He could so easily have found out about the questions I'd been asking. It was obvious to both of us after our first conversation that there was a reasonable possibility of his organisation taking over Logan Holdings. It was a logical development, and with me to help him it was quite easy. Besides, I knew that there was something about Daintry which would appeal to Conrad and make him lend the weight of his authority to the whole proceeding. But of course Daintry knew. He let me use him because he wanted to use me, but he must have known perfectly well that I was doing it because I wanted revenge on my brother (my younger brother, remember) for having done better than I did in the family firm by sucking up to Conrad and posing as the honest reliable alternative to slippery me.

'I got my revenge, and my position of power over all the people who had failed to back me when they had the chance. That was good. But all the time Daintry despised me, and used me, and kept me out of his inner councils. So though I had a little power he spoilt it for me.

'In the years after the takeover I worked incredibly hard. I hardly thought of anything else. I neglected Serena. When I came home I was too tired to do anything except drink and go to bed. I drank much too much during all that time. Serena was always out, pursuing her social career, being pursued by Bunny Hayford. We drifted apart. Then when she saw the way it was going, and that I was going to bite the hand that had been feeding me, she thought it was time to get out.

'Not that she knew *how* I was going to bite—she just knew the way my mind was working. You probably don't

86

know this, but in a really big organisation, which by then Daintry Enterprises had become, your entire time can be taken up by internal intrigue. In so far as you give any time at all to the supposed function of the organisation, it is only as a gambit in this endlessly complicated and intensely bitter struggle for position. The Americans are better at it than we are, but we're learning. English people tend to have a respect for hierarchies—it's probably something to do with the prefect system—but we're breeding it out. The Americans don't have it, and they don't have stiff upper lips either. The upper rungs of the ladder in the average large American firm are a riot of clinging shoving mouthing shrieking blubbering assassins; it's amusing when you first come across it, but gets a bit repetitive.

'Anyway, whether by learning from our new American associations or what, the enlarged Daintry Enterprises became adept at this particular game, and Daintry showed himself quite skilled at taking advantage of it. When we started going into the electronics field—he having quite rightly decided that then was the moment to go in, what with automation coming and so on—he took advantage of one of my private vendettas (I won't bore you with the details) to leave me in charge of one of the electronics firms and thereby, because of the rules of the holding company, lose me my seat on the main board. After that I had to get him into trouble, didn't I?

' "Rubbish," you say, putting on your cross face. But it is not rubbish. The trouble with you is that you have led a sheltered life (oh how angry you are by now) and know nothing of human nature. You are like a visitor from another world. You say, "On the moon all the mothers love their children so much that they grow up to love everybody else." That's as may be. We do things differently here.'

Dora could stand on her hind legs in the larder of the cottage and reach the egg-box, gently nose open the lid and extract an egg, unbroken. Once or twice she carried a whole box out into the garden and spent an hour or so taking out the eggs and playing with them, cavorting about with one in her mouth before abandoning it somewhere in the garden, still unbroken, and going back for another. It was a game which Agatha tried to discourage, but the habit of keeping the eggs on the bottom shelf of the larder was so strong that she often forgot to put them higher.

She could remember sitting on the back doorstep in the sun, the children scuffing with sticks in the dusty remains of what had been a gravel path, drawing houses. Beside her was an egg-box which she had recovered with four eggs still inside it. One of the others had disappeared and one was still in Dora's mouth. Agatha was too lazy to do more than scold. Dora danced about on the grass, making movements with her head as if she were throwing the egg up into the air and catching it again, although it was really still held in the delicate clasp of her teeth: perhaps becoming aware of Agatha's inattention, she trotted up to the doorstep, curling back her upper lip and groaning some sort of invitation to the game.

'No, Dora.'

Agatha held out her hand.

Dora gently deposited the egg in it.

'D'you see how she doesn't even crack them?' She held the egg out for George to see. It lay in the palm of her hand, warm and unblemished. 'How carefully she must have carried it. When I die I'll leave you an egg like that, dropping it into the palm of your hand uncracked, with all the stuff of life still in it.'

The sound of Lucy's stick in the gravel reminded her of Italy, of waking in the morning to the sound of a man hoeing in stony ground.

'I hope it will be cooked,' said George. When the white of his boiled egg was not quite solid, that he hated.

Sally was wearing a shiny green dress. Across the front was a frill of the same material which dipped under her arms and plunged almost to her waist at the back. At the hem, which was higher in the front than at the back, the same line was repeated by another frill which swayed and rustled round her when she walked. She had matching shiny green shoes with pointed toes, very high heels, and ankle straps. Round her neck she wore a shiny green ribbon with a cameo brooch pinned to the front of it. Her lips and nails were a wet-looking scarlet. She wore a golden bracelet from which dangled dark brown semi-precious stones.

'Black pearls, are they? Pretty—mn,' said the tall young man with sticking-out ears. He seemed to speak through his nose, hardly moving his lips at all, as he bent forward to peer at the bracelet.

'Of course,' said Sally, turning her wrist from side to side, slowly because of the glass of champagne she was holding.

'Of course,' agreed the young man, returning to the height from which he had come. His little eyes directed their feeble gaze down the long organ through which his frail tones appeared to emerge (eugenically speaking, his breeding was a disaster). 'What else could they be?' He gave a short quasi-experimental snicker.

'What indeed?' said Sally, rolling her eyes rather wildly. They lighted to her relief on the face of Joe Hertz, half turned away from her, talking in a group of people. 'Hullo,' she said breathlessly, laying a hand on his shoulder. He turned, looking rather startled.

'Do you know—?' She waved vaguely in the direction of the tall young man, but already a determined couple

89

making their way from one side of the room to the other had interposed themselves. 'Thank God for that. What a nightmare person.'

Joe, effectively detached from his previous conversation, looked at her attentively, as if waiting for further explanation.

'Why *do* I come to cocktail parties?' she said. She looked as if she really wanted to know.

'Because you're always afraid you might be missing something,' he answered firmly.

'That's it.' She glowed at him, as if no one had ever understood her before. 'But every time I find I'm not.'

'But the one time you didn't come he might be here, tossing his raven locks with impatience, jewels winking on his princely breast, waiting to sweep you up in front of him on his white horse and gallop out of the room and down the stairs and away over the burning sands of Arabia.'

'Not much room for a horse in here,' she said, looking round with a dissatisfied glance.

'He'd leave it downstairs then, tethered to the bannisters, jingling its bits and things. You'd know you'd been right to come as soon as you saw it there. You'd hurry up the stairs with your heart a-flutter.'

'You mustn't laugh at me for having a commonplace mind,' she said. But she looked quite happy about it.

He knew her only slightly, as a pretty girl who normally had more exciting people than him to talk to at parties. He also knew her to be in some way or other involved with Henry. He had not wanted to know this, for various rather complicated reasons, but it had not been possible to maintain his ignorance; common acquaintances asked him what was going on, as the close friend who might be expected to know, and besides Agatha and Henry were both thinner, and evenings with them were sometimes different from the old days, not so much when there was the odd sharp word as when they treated each other too delicately, as if they were both convalescent from an illness which each knew might in the case of the other recur and prove fatal: this sad tenderness had struck him more than once as a bad sign. Brian, a wordly friend, had said it was bound to happen from time to time, Henry being the sort of person he was: Agatha would have to adjust herself, he said. Joe supposed this to be true but wondered how, in practical day-to-day terms, one did adjust oneself, and knew that it was fear of just that kind of harsh necessity which made him a coward himself in personal relationships, a coward who depended on other people's successes in those directions for his own precarious sense of security.

Sally represented trouble, but he did not feel that he knew enough about her to know whether he ought to blame her for that.

'Have you got a car?' she asked.

'Yes. Do you want a lift?'

'If you could just drop me at the nearest taxi-rank it would be too marvellous. We're miles from anywhere here, aren't we?'

Smiling at this description of their hosts' rather fashionable address, he led the way out of the room, only to find that she had not followed him and was nowhere to be seen. He went downstairs and waited for quite a long time. She came at last, with a token apology. It turned out that she was supposed to be going on to another party but could not be bothered—or perhaps the party was mythical. Anyway they went to have dinner in Soho, at a quiet restaurant he liked where the food was good. She said in answer to his question that she had been there before, and then hesitated. At once he wished he had not asked her, because he had taken Henry there more than once and it was just the sort of quiet place, unfrequented by their friends, to which Henry might have taken Sally.

'With Henry.'

It had been too late to stop her saying it, but at least he could ignore it.

'What will you have?'

But he could not put it off for ever, and by the time it came, about halfway through the meal, food and wine and her pretty face and friendly talk had made him less reluctant.

'You're a great friend of Henry's, aren't you?' she said.

He might even be going to enjoy it. He had been a little nervous about that too. It smacked of betrayal.

'They're both my best friends,' he said sternly.

'You don't mind my talking about it?' she asked humbly.

He shook his head.

Her tale unfolded, with pauses for encouragement. She would rather die than break up the marriage. That was why she had insisted that all physical relations should cease some time ago. He was not quite sure whether to believe either of the two protestations. Certainly it appeared that she herself very much wanted to believe the first, but she left him a succession of openings for telling her she was wrong. Was the marriage not perhaps anyway doomed to failure, were they not too disparate in temperament in spite of their affection for each other and for the children, did Henry not need a different kind of person, more easy-going, extravert, sociable?

At one moment he looked down at his plate, struggling to control one of those foolish smiles that look like the beginnings of a childish crying fit, because he was curiously and conflictingly moved, and because he was also almost pityingly amused by his own reaction, by the fact that he was sitting opposite her in a warm sweat of anxiety, mechanically putting into his mouth from time to time food which tasted like blotting paper or wine which he gulped too thirstily so that the effect of it added to his general feeling of being about to start giving out some sort of buzzing sound. What shook him was the understanding which came to him while she was speaking of how much his own stability was bound up with that of the marriage of his two friends. Hearing it undermined from a vantage point so different from his own, and with an authority so convincing (because in certain ways she must of course know Henry better than he did, which in itself was a disturbing thought), seemed to be giving him a push towards an independence which he had not known he lacked. It was alarming, but there was also a sense of liberation, and so of excitement. As Sally talked on and on, exposing without any hesitation or embarrassment all sorts of intimacies which he could not imagine any man of his acquaintance revealing in such a way, there were present in his mind not only various straightforward regrets about the whole thing, not only a natural curiosity, but other vaguer, less accountable emotions. It meant that these two were not so much better than he was after all, if the relationship which not only he among their friends had envied could so founder. Was this at last something which Henry could not get away with? Was Agatha's wholeness to be splintered, leaving her weak, accessible? If she should fall into his arms in search of comfort, was that not what he had really always wanted? And if that should annoy Henry, was that not too what he had always wanted?

While he listened, and said 'Yes' and 'No' and 'I see', he was recognising the involved considerations which might affect his own imaginable behaviour, and then he was realising that some kind of moral fastidiousness in himself would make such behaviour no more than a possibility, would make him dismiss it in fact as insufficiently serious; but the fact that he had even recognised the possibility bore out his view of himself, that he was not fundamentally a very nice person.

As he usually did when he despaired of himself, he focussed his attention on someone else.

'Now wait a minute,' he said. 'Let's just look at you.'

He looked at her.

'You're very pretty.'

She smiled doubtfully.

'Now let's see.'

He went on looking at her, with his elbows on the table and his chin resting on his clasped hands.

'How old were you when you first had a lover?'

'Seventeen,' she said, accepting the invitation to tell him the story of her life.

Her father was a successful surgeon, her mother, she said, conventional and boring—'not that we don't get on exactly, we just haven't much in common.' At sixteen she had gone to a finishing-school in London where she took a course in modelling and began to be photographed for magazines. She went to work for a fashionable photographer with whom she fell in love, worked incredibly hard, learnt, she said, everything she knew; but he was not kind, he treated all his girl-friends badly; to escape, she became involved with a rich young man whose family thought she was not good enough for him; he was so sweet, they were so mean, he had a nervous breakdown, chased her with a knife, threw her down the stairs. 'Gosh,' said Joe. But she seemed to have quite enjoyed it. Now here she was, a successful model, earning a lot of money, asked to smart parties, pursued by this and that handsome, rich or famous man. Henry, she said, was 'real', the others were not. Her life was useless, she felt, her activities trivial, she had no purpose. He had seen her photographed with Lord Marner. Yes, well, of course, that was really quite funny. Her solemnity disappeared as she began to repeat the indiscretions of Johnny Marner, with which apparently he regaled her every morning on the telephone; as like as not a bunch of flowers from him would arrive even as they were talking, for that was the sort of person he was. Of course the whole thing was quite ridiculous, and she wouldn't dream of letting the affair go any further, but at the same time it was so funny, and he was rather sweet in a way and had such lovely manners and took her to such lovely places. 'Do you see at all what I mean?'

He saw. He saw the symmetrical oval of her delicately coloured face, her black-lashed, pearly-painted eyes, the controlled smooth gold of her swept back hair: a phenomenon. Following an idea of her which was beginning to come to him, he imagined a context of cool rooms impeccably furnished, of pale-skinned odalisques who were prodigies of wit and savoir-faire, of black panthers lounging on cushions, sapphires, subtle lights, infinite afternoons. He began to smile.

'Go on,' he said. 'What else?'

Marner had taken her to stay with a duke. She had noticed everything.

'You're marvellous. You're very clever, do you know that? Go on.'

Oh, but it was all so silly, so unreal. Of course he was rather powerful and was always telling Cabinet Ministers to pull themselves together and calling up smooth chauffeur-driven cars from nowhere. He had asked her to go on some shooting party in Alsace. Of course she was not going. Although it would have been nice to meet the King of Bavaria or at least the man who would have been King of Bavaria if there had been a King of Bavaria. 'But you shouldn't encourage me. You're as bad as Henry. He always wants to hear what he calls amazing tales. I used to think it was because he wanted me to find someone else, so that he'd be rid of me. But only the other day he said something very strange to me, about wanting me to like his

95

children. He's never said anything like that before.'

'No, no,' said Joe. His mind was quite made up. 'You don't want the dreariness of domestic life. You want luxury, love, beautiful things, expensive things, adventure, intrigue. You're a perfect beautiful marvellous specimen of a good-time girl, a courtesan.'

She looked shocked, but there was no stopping him. He had seen a solution and was going to put all his professional skill into selling it.

'People don't know how to live any more,' he said earnestly. 'This is the age of the drab and the dreary and the conformist and the average man. Our whole society is suffering from guilt without knowing what to do about it, so we go on behaving in the same old way but less so, because we've lost confidence and so we don't dare to have any fun. You belong to a different age, an age when there was a proper place for someone like you, where all your talent for being beautiful, charming and pleasing to men could unfold and be adored. But you must let youself be what you are, choose yourself and become yourself, and not be ashamed of being unique.'

He paused for breath and refilled both their glasses. Sally was smiling, enjoying it. Encouraged, he went on.

'What an absurd idea it is that every woman only wants to get married and have children. Some do and some don't. Why should custom force them all to conform? You don't want to waste yourself on one man, cooking, washing, darning, changing babies' nappies, all your lustre dimmed. All right, in ten years, when you feel the moment has come for a little calm, a little routine, you might, with every possible inducement in the way of ease, independence and scope for creating something perfect, agree to settle down. But in the meantime—'

'Yes?'

'You create something perfect. Yourself. Certainly you

96

meet the King of Bavaria. In a man-made world you learn from men in order to turn yourself into a unique woman. Thus you conquer them. But you are kind, discreet, wise. You do not feature in divorce cases. You bring pleasure, not pain; wherever you go you confer an inestimable benefit just by being there. In a certain world you will become famous. A small world. But your name will be mentioned in the history books.'

'You *are* funny. How do I start?'

'This shooting party. When is it?'

'Next month.'

'I may be going to Paris about then. I've been offered a job by an American advertising firm which would mean living in Paris. I probably shan't take it but I could go over and talk to them about it. I'll meet you there. It will be a good thing if you leave independently of Lord Marner. It will show that you're not to be considered as completely attached to him. You're meeting a friend in Paris. A little mysterious. Do you know Paris?'

She shook her head. 'I spent a day there once being photographed for *Vogue*.'

He nodded seriously. 'We must see about that.'

'You mean you're going to train me up somehow. Well, that's all right, I suppose. But you'll have to see it through, you know. You can't give me up halfway.' She spoke teasingly, as if the whole fantasy was still a joke.

'I shan't give you up. I'm going to take an interest in you, you see.'

They developed the fantasy. It went very nicely. They had an amusing evening and were left with the feeling that something had started, though both were vague as to what it really was. Sally pretended to treat it all as a joke, but it was she who was more serious. There was no doubt that she would now accept the invitation to the shooting party.

Joe went home cheerful and rather drunk. He lived in a

97

sort of bachelors' rooming-house on the borders of Pimlico and Belgravia. Because he thought himself always on the point of leaving London he had never bothered to find himself anywhere more agreeable. He went upstairs rather noisily and let himself into his room, which was neater than might have seemed possible in view of the number of books it contained.

'I really like her,' he said, undressing rather unsteadily and folding his clothes carefully before putting them on the chair. 'I really like her.'

In his pyjamas he gazed into the mirror above the washbasin.

'Why not? A role for her. A role for me. Best for Agatha. Best for Henry.'

He squeezed some toothpaste onto his toothbrush.

'Wonders. I'll do wonders with her.'

He cleaned his teeth, put the toothbrush back into the mug and the top onto the toothpaste, and got into bed.

'I would do anything for Agatha. Agatha, I remember your face as the heaving tides remember the moon.'

He put his head onto his pillow and noticed that it seemed to be heaving very slightly too.

'She'll have to wait until I get back from Hungary of course.'

He reached out for the light-switch, fumbled, found it. He turned out the light and fell asleep.

Conrad could not sleep. Suffering from flatulence and uncontrollable anxiety, propped up on his pillows, he tried to read Herodotus, sipping Bisodol.

He hated his bedroom at the flat. It was too small. On the other hand service flats within walking distance of the Houses of Parliament were almost impossible to find, and staying at the Club was not the same as having one's own rooms. Besides, there was Jess, who was used to the flat and to spending long hours alone there. Snoring now in her basket beside his bed, she added to his anxieties. He shrank from the pain her death, which could not now be long delayed, must cause him; nor had he a successor in view. She had had puppies but he had kept none, thinking she might have another litter, and then what with one thing and another she never had, so there was no young dog to take her place and though he could find a puppy he wanted the same breeding as near as possible, and that might be hard to find. He wrote on the pad of paper which he kept on the bedside table, 'Coombs, re puppy,' which reminded him of Agatha and the beagle which had been run over. There was no doubt it had been an excellent little bitch, that. Bad luck, it had been. If only Agatha wasn't so difficult, he could have given her another one. He would willingly have done it, would have enjoyed it, traced the breeder, found a sibling, it would have been a nice thing to have done; but it was just that sort of pleasant interchange which Agatha's attitude made so difficult.

'Not very co-operative,' Skarrett had said that evening on the telephone. That was Agatha all right. He had thought of having another word with Imogen after that telephone call but could get no answer from her flat, even at half-past eleven. How she managed to hold down a job, keeping such late hours, he could not imagine. He would have to try and catch her in the morning. He had a feeling about Agatha, that was all, but his feelings were usually right.

'Unlike me not to be able to sleep,' he said aloud.

He put down his book and went to the window. Pulling aside the curtain, he saw a line of pale light at the edge of the sky. It was already dawn. He really had had a sleepless night.

The telephone rang.

He picked up the receiver.

'Yes?'

'You asked me to let you know when we got the Egyptian answer in. It came about an hour ago.'

'Rejecting our ultimatum of course.'

'Yes.'

'Ah.'

'As expected.'

'Quite.'

'So we proceed.'

'Yes. Well, thanks for letting me know, old chap. The next ten days or so won't be much fun, will they?'

'No.'

'We'll pull through though, I daresay. You must be tired, William. I won't keep you. Many thanks again. Goodbye.'

He put down the receiver.

'Pity,' he said, sitting on the edge of the bed.

He swung his legs up and pulled the bedclothes over them.

'We seem to have been swept into rather a rash adventure,' he said, arranging his pillows. At the same time he was conscious that the multifarious anxieties which had been keeping him awake were sliding away from him as if under the influence of a beneficent drug.

Now we shall have to close our ranks, he thought, and fell asleep.

Agatha dreamed about Italy. It had been raining and she was standing in front of the door to the tower house, which had a rough grey stone architrave set into the variegated stones of the wall above it. There were two large grey stones, each a natural pillar, on either side of the door. Last summer she had taken a photograph of the two children standing in the dark doorway. 'Look sad,' she had said and they had, like little refugees. In her dream it was Orlando who was standing there, in the shadow so that she could hardly see him. He was leaning against one of the grey stones and she had the impression that he was ill. 'You haven't maintained it,' he was saying, and though his voice was weak it conveyed an awful urgency. 'You haven't maintained it.' But she knew he did not mean the building.

In the grassy space by the well Henry, wearing a smart suit, was jiving with Marilyn Monroe, backwards and forwards on skilful fast feet, twirling her under his outstretched arm, and she was smiling rapturously; of course, Agatha thought in her dream, that is only right and proper, and she knew that Orlando thought so too. But this business of the maintenance, that was her concern.

Just before she woke another place, very sharply defined, superimposed itself for an instant, a place on an island with blue sea far below. The sunlight was extraordinarily clear—had she ever been there?—there were columns, an ancient ruin, very white and quiet, two broken columns, in the space between which she was going to put something, but had lost it, or forgotten what it was.

'She's taken it. I put it in its special place and she's taken it.'

'Taken what, darling?' she said as she woke up.

It was George, in his pyjamas.

'I put it in the special drawer I always keep it in and Lucy's taken it.' He was indignant; more than that, shocked. 'Just taken it. My second-best red pencil.'

Conrad was on the telephone at eight o'clock in spite of his restless night.

'Charles Edwards, the ex-burglar.' He had dialled Inspector Skarrett's private number. 'He was an acquaintance of Paul's and could have put him on to whoever it was who arranged the escape. It might have been him rather than the Russians—after all Paul was never really one of their men so far as we know. I just give you that idea for what it's worth.'

'I won't bore you with the technical details,' wrote Paul. 'But this little rather rude-looking thing we were making was tremendously useful, not to say pretty well essential, if you were building an atomic reactor. Of course it had other functions as well and I didn't myself appreciate its more thrilling potentialities until I had a mysterious message from someone called Colonel Longfellow who wanted me to meet him for a drink in the Grosvenor Hotel of all places. I feared the worst (my past is even murkier than you think) but I went along and there he was all lean and military with a macintosh and a whisky and soda, and so I said, "You must be from M.I.5" and he was *furious*. I can tell them a mile off. He wanted to know what foreigners were buying the thing and if they were would I pretend I personally had to supervise the installation and have a snoop round at the same time to see who was making atom bombs on the quiet. So we sat there in our armchairs with our whiskies and sodas being tremendously confidential and responsible and officer class together when all the time he must have known I wasn't in the least like that. I mean they have dossiers on everybody, these people, and he must have known what a frightful officer I was and how only Uncle Conrad's influence prevented me from being prosecuted for that unfortunate little incident in the Leicester Square public lavatory. The silly thing was one was meant to do it all for patriotic motives, and I needed money. I'd made absurdly generous arrangements for Serena at the divorce, I'd spent too much on living it up a bit here and there after she left, and I was being black-mailed. (Under the quaint law we have, by which you can be sent to prison for having sex with a man—well, *you* can't obviously, but I can—most homosexuals are black-mailed most of the time). So I began to think. If this thing was so interesting perhaps the countries to which it was a prohibited export might like it, and perhaps they might pay for it.

'I knew how to get hold of them. It was all to do with my murky past again. I was actually a member of the Communist party for a short time. You didn't know that, did you? Quite a flirtation with politics I had, after the war. But I could see nothing was going to happen. The English will never turn Communist, they're such snobs. An English Communist could have a duke at gunpoint: if he asked him to stay for the weekend he'd drop the gun and dash off to Moss Bros to hire a dinner-jacket. It could only come by foreign conquest, and I couldn't see that happening for some time, so I rather slid out of the whole thing. But I knew a lot of spies. Incidentally I knew Burgess and Maclean too—well, Burgess really, but that was through drinking clubs more—and I can tell you *that* story's not over yet. Anyway, nothing was easier than to make contact with the people I needed. And of course they wanted my little gadget and a great deal more besides. My guess is—but I may be wrong—that they knew a good deal about how to make the things anyway: whether they had spies in the factory already or whether it was just that their own people were working along parallel lines I don't know, but I had the feeling that they were just playing me along about that and that what they were much more interested in was exactly how many we were supplying to the British Government, and where. I made them wait for that, which was O.K. in one way because they put the price up, but in another it may have been my downfall because I had to meet them too often. I don't know what made our people suspicious—perhaps the M.I.5 man wasn't quite such a fool as I thought him—anyway when I saw a man reading the paper in a parked car outside my house two mornings running I went to Charlie at once. I believe in insurance. There's a perfectly efficient organisation for getting you out of prison if you're prepared to pay. It's expensive, I know, but worth it, I think you'll agree. My charming hostess this morning vouchsafed a remark while handing me my foul breakfast. "He says you're to be ready to leave," she said. What does he think I am? I've never been readier to leave anywhere in my life. So I said with heavy irony, "I'll start my packing," but she just padded out with her disgusting slippers. If she's not careful I'll leave her something nasty in the bed.'

'They know.'
Imogen's face was perfectly, startlingly, white.
'Sit down.' Agatha pulled forward a chair and with a hand on Imogen's arm firmly sat her down in it.
'They know, Agatha,' said Imogen again.
Agatha looked round quickly. Miss Bannister was in the back room and Miss Wickham, who had seen Imogen's desperately hurried arrival, was tactfully bent over her embroidery at the other end of the shop.
Agatha, having given her chair to Imogen, sat down on the edge of the table and said, 'What happened?'
'They came to see me again, and they know. It's no good. You'll have to tell them, Agatha.'
'Who came to see you?'
'That Inspector.'
'What did he say?'
'He knows about Charlie Edwards and that he arranged Paul's escape and that you gave them money.'
'What did he say exactly?'
'He said he knew Charlie Edwards had arranged it.'
'Charlie Edwards didn't arrange it. It was a friend of his.'

'It's the same thing,' said Imogen impatiently. The colour was coming back into her cheeks now that the horrifying moment of breaking the news to Agatha was over. 'It's no good, Agatha. You'll have to go and see them.'

'Of course I'm not going to go and see them,' said Agatha. 'Just tell me exactly what he said.'

'He said you must go and see him.'

'What did he say that he knew?'

'He said that he knew it was all to do with Charlie Edwards. He said it was only a matter of time until they found out all the details. He said that if you had given them any money you must go and tell him all about it at once, otherwise you'll certainly be caught and sent to prison.'

'*If* I had. He can't have known then.'

'He does know. It's no good. He does know.' She had turned white again.

Agatha looked at her. She has told him, she thought.

She stood up and walked slowly away, turned over a book on the top of a pile on one of the tables and walked back. She was fairly certain that Imogen must have told the Inspector everything she knew but she did not want her to have to say so. She would have liked to have embraced her sister, but they had never been demonstrative in that sort of way.

Instead she said, 'Don't worry. He may not know as much as he would like us to think. I'll wait for him to come to me.'

Imogen had screwed up her chiffon scarf into a ball and was turning it round and round in her hands.

'But if you go to him and tell him, it will be better for you. He said so.'

'I will do that if it seems the right thing. I don't think I ought to do it yet. Don't worry, it will be all right. Leave it to me.'

'But I don't want to leave it to you. I want to help you.'

To Imogen's anxious eyes it was as if Agatha visibly retreated and from a new distance said quietly, 'No, you can't do that.' Then she turned away, without seeing Imogen's immediate tears, and went into the back room where she said politely to Miss Bannister, 'I suppose there wouldn't be any chance of a cup of tea for my sister? She's had a bit of a shock.'

'Of course, my dear.' Miss Bannister at once rose to her feet and set about lighting the gas-ring.

'Tea? Oh goody,' said Miss Wickham, hurrying in from the shop and busily setting out the blue-striped mugs. 'Just what I need.'

They both assumed that Imogen was pregnant and felt very sorry for her, so pretty and so sad. Miss Bannister would have liked to contribute something towards the cost of an abortion, Miss Wickham had already determined to adopt the child. Fortunately both decided that their offers would be premature, and kept them in reserve.

Conrad walked briskly across St James's Park, with Jess at his heels. It was cold and misty but with a faint suggestion of sunshine through the mist and the smell of burning leaves on the air. He wondered if there had been a frost at Mount Sorrel. He hoped the crisis would not prevent him from getting down there for the weekend.

'Come along, Jess,' he said unnecessarily. He felt very well. 'Sometimes I think one sleeps too much,' he said, startling a middle-aged woman in a hat who happened to be walking in the opposite direction. 'An occasional shorage of sleep clears the mind.' He should not have hesitated so much about Agatha. She should be brought to her senses as quickly as possible and the wretched Paul caught and put away. He had told that Inspector it was time to get a move on. Really it was perfectly disgraceful that they hadn't found him already.

This evening the bombers would move in. Alert young men—he envied them in a way—their trained reflexes at work, their faculties stretched, coming in low at dusk to bomb the Egyptian airfields, a competent operation to put the places out of action, a definite move, a clear unequivocal statement. How much he had seen bungled by inaction: Italy in 1935, the Rhineland in 1936. 'You can't be too nice, you know, in this wicked world.' And though of course things changed and one had to move with the times, one couldn't help sympathising with people who thought the British should never have left Suez in the first place.

'Robust,' he said. 'We must be robust.' His feeling of well-being was so intense that as he walked along he held his arms in front of him and with his hands open horizontally rubbed the palms briskly together at the same time saying, 'Ho ho, ho ho, ho *ho.*'

Jess, delighted by the way things were going, broke into a lolloping canter. A smiling park attendant said cheerfully, 'Nice morning, sir!'

'Excellent, excellent,' answered Conrad.

Of course it was a nice morning. He was going to get a lot done today. He hoped there wouldn't be too much talking, he had a lot of other things to see to, letters to write, arrangements to make, he really wanted to find time to look at the new chrysanthemums in the Royal Horticultural Society's Autumn Show too. Still, he might have to let that go, if there was too much on.

'What an interesting life we lead, Jess, for a couple of old fogeys.'

Henry and Joe had lunch together.
'I had dinner with Sally last night.'
'Did you? How did that come about?'

'We were both at a boring party. She's marvellous, isn't she?'

Henry looked pleased but said deprecatingly, 'Not too bright of course.'

'No, she's quick though, funny.'

'I'm glad you liked her,' said Henry.

Joe felt from the easy way in which he spoke that he meant it, and this seemed significant. If Henry did not feel that there was anything that needed to be concealed about his friendship with Sally, presumably he himself no longer thought of it as dangerous. This augured well, Joe thought. For everything.

They talked about mutual friends, gossiping, before going back to the subject of Sally, and the behaviour of Lord Marner, and their joint curiosity about this enigmatic but grand figure.

'Incidentally,' said Henry changing the subject abruptly, 'do you know any really discreet solicitors? There's something I want to find out but I don't know who to ask.'

Joe wondered whether he had misjudged the situation. One never quite knew with Henry. On the other hand he had thought he did quite know.

Confused, he said, 'There's always poor old David Matthews.'

'Oh yes, so there is. Poor old David Matthews. Look here, could you ask him something for me? It's a bit difficult for me. Would you mind? Ask him what would be the sentence on someone who was caught giving money to a group of people who organised the escape from prison of someone who had been given a long sentence.'

'Cripes.'

'Supposing the person who had given the money to be a relation of the person who escaped.'

'Yes. Gosh.'

'All quite hypothetical of course.'

'It would probably be only a fine, wouldn't it?'
'Apparently not.'
'Oh Lord. I'll find out.'
'Just so that one knows.'
'Does it look like—um—being found out?'
'I'm not sure. I hope not.'
'So do I. Good Lord.'

He acted quickly. Late in the afternoon he telephoned Henry in his office. They met on a bench in St Paul's Churchyard. Joe unfolded a typewritten sheet of foolscap paper.

'You were quick,' said Henry.

'I stood over him while he rang up his friend in criminal law. This is what he says. "A person who harbours an offender under the Official Secrets Act commits a misdemeanour, and the maximum penalty on indictment is two years. I doubt whether the close relationship, or the fact of a first offence, would really be material. My feeling is that the Court would want to give the maximum sentence possible."'

'Why?' said Henry.

'I suppose espionage is considered a bad thing. And helping someone to evade the law. "The matter of bail would presumably be strongly opposed in the case of espionage, and so therefore the person concerned would in practice be starting his prison sentence from the date of arrest."'

'No bail,' said Henry.

They sat side by side on the bench in silence.

'So really,' said Henry thoughtfully, 'a certain line has been crossed. She has put herself on the other side of a certain line.'

'Yes.'

'Interesting. Thanks.' He stood up. 'You won't say anything, will you? Nothing may come of it, at least I hope not.'

He nodded, a little preoccupied, and walked away.

'Keep in touch,' said Joe anxiously. But Henry did not look round.

Joe walked back towards his office, wishing he could ride beside her, on a tired horse, with a tattered flag. When she swayed in her saddle, exhausted from the battle, he would slip to the ground and be at her side; no one else should support her to her tent and sleep across the entrance through the night while her resting soul renewed itself among its own vast ancient images; no one else in the morning should ride beside her when they went, refreshed, to renew the battle in the plain. Or he would stand up in court and plead for her life with such eloquence that the judge would weep. Then he felt ashamed, and wished his daydreams were not always about himself.

Henry suggested that Agatha should go to the cottage early.

'It will probably be the last time we can go before it gets too cold. Let George miss one day's school. They won't mind. He's only five. You take the car, and I'll come by train.'

'It seems rather extravagant,' said Agatha doubtfully.

'I can afford the fare for once. You can meet me at the station. It would do the children good to be there a bit longer this time.'

From his office he telephoned a neighbour of old Mrs Parker who lived in the village and sent a message asking her to go up to the cottage and light the fire and leave a few stores ready. She had done it before for them but they did not like to ask her too often because she was old and though she could sometimes get a lift from the woodmen, of whom her son was one, at other times she had to walk and it was a long way.

When Agatha arrived with the children and found the fire lit and everything made ready, she immediately thought, He must know that I am going to be caught. But it did not lessen her pleasure in the place.

She walked in the woods with the children, available to them in an emergency but in the meantime not listening. When Lucy said 'Mummy?' she said 'Mn?' but then Lucy forgot what she had been going to say or was interrupted by George. Sometimes Lucy said 'Mummy?' again as if she had something really important to say, and Agatha said 'Mn?' again, and again nothing transpired. It was a routine she was used to and in which she could fulfil her obligations without interrupting her train of thought. Possibly Lucy's train of thought was not interrupted either, always supposing that she had one. Her consciousness seemed still to be almost exclusively occupied by her reactions, often extravagant, to the immediate moment. George, being older, was more given to philosophising, and when he was alone with either of his parents for any length of time would produce in unhurried but continuous succession the results of his speculations, simple but well-formed concepts on most of the world's great questions, shining fishes from the clear waters of his mind. When he was with Lucy his conversation was on an altogether lower level. This afternoon they were being rabbits, with voices and sentiments of which any right-minded rabbit ought to have been ashamed. When the squeaks and baby talk penetrated to Agatha she said, 'Surely rabbits don't talk like that' in a shocked voice.

'They have witchy fluffy voices,' said Lucy sillily.

'For heaven's *sake*.'

But they had gambolled on ahead, stopping every now and then to waggle their bottoms, which presumably had witchy fluffy tails on them, and Agatha waited until they were out of earshot before following them down the field, hoping that by the time she caught up with them they might have moved on to some less objectionable fantasy.

They were going down to the old Timberwork mill, where the children liked climbing on the ruined walls. It was the first time they had been that way since Dora's death. The fact that Dora had been run over coalesced in her mind with her feeling that Henry must know more than she did about the police enquiry, and produced in her a feeling, not unfamiliar, of her own inadequacy, of there being really nothing else for her to do but take things quietly: she knew that there was a certain sense in which as far as the outside world was concerned she really had no idea how to behave. Henry, on the other hand, had.

The rough wood on the slope above the mill was neglected. Branches which had fallen in last winter's winds had not been cleared away for firewood: the undergrowth was thick and the paths hard to find. It was as if Conrad had not the heart to apply his science there, so near the scene of former disappointments. Elsewhere his woods were beautifully tended, his timber-growing a serious business. Rides were kept clear between plantations, the trees thinned and pruned; but here a thin uprooted wych-elm could lean across the path, held from falling completely by the branches of other trees which supported too a huge growth of old man's beard, whose abundance looked from a distance like a great fall of soft grey roses. Agatha paused, near a tangle of brambles from which a month or two earlier she had picked enough fruit for six pounds of blackberry jelly. She looked for late remnants but after the recent frosts there was nothing. She stood still and could just hear the children's voices. They had run on so far that they might already be down at the bottom, at the mill. Their voices came to her with a slight echo. Otherwise there was no sound except a gentle continuous rustling, so much like rain falling on the trees that she looked up towards the grey sky; but it was only the last yellowish leaves falling all round her, singly and slowly through the damp windless air. Here all was well. For once she did not feel out of place.

She liked the feeling of her trousers over her stomach, pulled tight by her hands being in her pockets; the longer strides she had to take because her boots were rather big: by such little things could messages of liberty be conveyed; also by the touch of damp air on her cheeks, the smell of leaves, moss, fungus, the slow sound of cawing rooks. Her sense of isolation was acceptable here, but must never be relished because that would be pride. There were so many errors into which she might fall, and the God in whom she did not believe had been besought for forgiveness so much lately that it had become a habit to have the words always somewhere near the topmost layer of her mind. If she were to be run over crossing a road she would die with such a shriek of 'Oh forgive me!' that everyone would be left wondering what horrible crime she had committed, not knowing how private were her sins.

One of them she had recently diagnosed for herself as displaced jealousy. Never having allowed herself to feel jealousy of Sally—or perhaps it would be more accurate to say, having most vigorously rejected, because it seemed to her so horrible, her jealousy of Sally—she had allowed the snake she held to recoil and feed on her restraining arm. That is to say, as well as the lowering of morale consequent upon her husband's having fallen in love with someone else she was suffering from an extra anxiety and self-hate which came from her absolute refusal to hate the husband and the someone else. She guessed that by now; and since she knew that the worst was over, that it was largely a question of time, of all three living it down, she sometimes consciously tried to dismiss Henry as selfish, Sally as vain and frivolous, by cursing them aloud. It did no good.

It was easier to believe the fault lay in her own over-estimate of what was to be expected from marriage. She had thought of it as some kind of Holy Grail, in the quest for which, that is to say in the daily renewal of the attempt to do it perfectly, self would be transcended and the soul satisfied. She could see that might be a terrible bore for someone who just wanted to be comfortable. She had no right to be demanding, must therefore adapt. But if, in adapting, a certain amount had to go, what was she left with? Her work was to rear her children, but to lose herself in them would be wrong, not to say impossible, feeling as she did the weight of her own personality. What else? These dripping woods.

She remembered reading about some clever person who had gone to Oxford or Cambridge at a young age and lived in keen daily expectation of meeting the really brilliant people. After a year or so he realised that the really brilliant people were himself and his friends: it was a severe disillusionment In adult life Agatha had looked for the visions and the certainties; perhaps the visions and the certainties were only the vague intimations of her childhood. Which brought her back to the Mount Sorrel woods. And to those intimations for which she often had to wait so long and which alone had the power to renew themselves.

'Parthenogenesis,' she said, pronouncing the word pedantically, walking downhill now quite fast, her gum-boots flumping against her legs, her hands till in her pockets. 'Love must commit parthenogenesis.'

She took her hands out of her pockets and began to run.

When she reached the mill she found that the children were climbing up the most dangerous part of the ruins, behind the mill, where the drawing offices and the canteen had been built onto the more solid eighteenth-century structure in about 1932. This part was mostly a heap of rubble now—willow herb and buddleia had had time to take a hold, a few rank elders too—but a couple of walls were still standing and there was scope for climbing.

'Be careful,' said Agatha but she did not call them down. She knew that Lucy would never pass George, and that George was really quite cautious. Little stones fell, dislodged.

'Careful,' said Lucy, losing her bravado.

If it should be necessary for me to wear an anonymous overall, thought Agatha, sitting down on a stone, and sew hemp with a huge needle in a line of other women, and be in a place where there is always the sound of echoing footsteps and clanging doors and perhaps shrieks, will it make me less ignorant or shall I not be able to bear it? A lot of women did it at the time of the suffragettes and they were not exactly criminals any more than I am. But I have such bruises in my heart where I feel for my children, I cannot bear much pain in that particular area.

She thought she remembered hearing that it always smelt of urine in prison. Every morning she would have to tear open with bleeding fingers the iron curtains which would have closed over her heart in the night, because if once she left them closed she would have failed. But she had had a little practice.

'Listen, children.' It would be easy to prepare them now. She knew she could do it with such confidence that they would be able to accept it, in the easy way of children, but she did not want to do it unless she was more sure than she was at the moment that it would be necessary. 'Listen. I've got a good idea. We'll go back by the village and buy some doughnuts for tea. Then we'll go home and make the house really warm and I'll tell you a

long story.'
    'Really long?'
    'Really long.'
    Because although she was full of doubt and difficulty she
was at the same time so strong she was sometimes afraid of
breaking things just by looking at them, which was why
she had to be especially careful to make sure that her
glance should be benign.

    'By the time you get this,' wrote Paul, on a dark after-
noon—only half-past two and already it felt like evening,
the air through the window, which he was keeping open
now through claustrophobia, soft with rain and milder
than lately, bearing a faint smell of the bonfires in surrounding back gardens where the fallen leaves and uprooted weeds smouldered after the weekend's work; not
that the house he was in had anything to contribute in that
way, having sacrificed its garden to the structure in which
he found himself, the doubtful advantage of the spare
bedroom—'I shall be on the move. You can think of me as
feeling a physical weight removed, the weight of this foul
little house, these pebble-papered walls, my thoughts. I've
had enough.
    'I got her to buy me an envelope and a stamp and when
they come to fetch me the first thing I'll do will be to find
a post-box, then you'll know I'm on my way out of the
country—they seemed to think when they were bringing
me here it would be by boat but they don't tell me much—
I don't want to know really, just so long as they get me
out. She came in yesterday and said, "He says tomorrow or
the next day." I'm afraid I lost my nerve for the first time,
I screamed at her, or at least I started to scream and then
I remembered the neighbours so I whispered—I said,
"Tell him he bloody makes it tomorrow or I'll kill him,"
and all that sort of stuff; rather shaming, I suppose, but

it's dying a slow death being in this room. I said, "Tell him my sister will give him some more money if he makes it tomorrow instead of the next day." I hope to God there wasn't anyone in the next-door house who could have heard, I think they go out all day. You won't mind if he comes to you for more money, will you? It's that or madness, I can tell you. Not that he will, I'm sure he was going to come today anyway.

'So when you get this you'll know it's worked and I haven't had to use my last resort. Oh yes, I've got that too, I thought of everything. I bloody nearly used it yesterday too—darkest hours before dawn and all that. I thought they were coming, you see, and when she said tomorrow or the next day I thought, rather a quick death than this slow one, and I nearly swallowed the thing. But I didn't. And if you get this letter we can both forget about all that because it will be a letter of triumph, won't it?

'Thanks for getting me out. I couldn't have stood it. I'm not very strong in any way. You know that. Other people haven't always known it because of my cutting tongue. But if people always treat you as if you were nasty, what can you do but pretend you're being nasty on purpose?

'You on the other hand are beginning to get a reputation for being nice. So you'll be able to pretend you're being nice on purpose. But I know you're not really all that nice. You're too strong, for one thing. You try to tone yourself down all the time, don't you, so as not to intimidate people. But I know. You'd like to gather everything and everyone into your own atmosphere and make them be happy in your own way—you're so sure its the only right one. That's why Henry has to get away from you sometimes, to breathe another atmosphere. You think he's a rat for being unfaithful to you. He has to, to keep the balance. You're too bossy, even though you never say a word.

'I've always been very perceptive. The trouble is I've so far missed my vocation. I ought to have been a writer, a novelist. Novelists have always been a venal lot, never outstanding for moral worth, often dishonest, certainly vain, silly, self-centred, snobbish and peculiar in their sexual habits. I should be perfectly convincing as a novelist. So as well as a sort of semi-fictionalised autobiography—more or less a new form I've worked out, a bit like Christopher Isherwood with a dash of Virginia Woolf—and perhaps those articles for *Encounter* that I told you about, I'm going to do a comic novel—Evelyn Waugh rather—which incidentally will be a *roman à clef* showing up Conrad's hypocrisy—and that in itself will be rather a lark because it will appear under a pseudonym and won't half set people guessing. Then of course we can leak out the sensational truth. I mean, I might as well cash in on my unsought fame, mightn't I? I thought of the plot last night —I haven't been sleeping well—it just about saved me from the abyss of despair, I can tell you—and now I'm full of optimism again as you can see—they can't keep me down. To add a bit of spice I'm giving Conrad an incestuous relationship with our mother, but otherwise it's all true, virtually. I'm going to have a—'

But there were footsteps on the stairs. He listened. Police. Two policemen. Heavy feet. A pause. The door quietly opened.

'They're here,' she said.

He was white.

'Why?'

'To take you.'

'Who?'

She stepped aside and the men in belted overcoats came in.

'Time to go.'

118

'Thank God. I thought you were the police.'

He scrawled on the bottom of the page, his hand shaking violently, 'They've come—in haste—imagine my joy—Paul.'

He folded the bulky letter clumsily and was stuffing it into the envelope as he followed the man out of the room and down the stairs.

Conrad had never much liked Penelope Waring. He thought of her as one of Judith's worldly friends, and tried to forget that at one time she had also been a friend of Orlando's, and that indeed when he had first met Orlando he had appeared to be some kind of protégé of Penelope's. It was a long time ago. When one was young one had relationships with women whom one did not necessarily exactly like. Before one was married of course. The fact that in Orlando's case one had had a few relationships with women one might or might not exactly have liked after one was married was an inconvenience Conrad was not prepared to entertain. More and more he found loose morals hard to tolerate. He tried to tolerate them—he believe it his Christian duty to do so—but he really rather hated all that sort of thing. Why did people not concentrate on doing a useful job of work instead? Even his occasional visits to the select establishment in Curzon Street which, undertaken at first from loneliness and need, had come to be no more than a precaution against some kind of imaginable charge at Heaven's gate of having been a prig, were now very rare indeed. So there were one or two aspects of periods of Orlando's life—aspects which had never anyway been obtrusive, since Orlando had not been the kind of person thoughtlessly to give offence—which Conrad preferred to forget. Orlando was his friend; Alexandra, the Field-Marshal's daughter, his short-lived love. They were all he had in the way of the deepest affections and he was not going to let the memory of either be spoilt.

It was for Orlando's sake that he went to Penelope Waring's cocktail party, because for Orlando's sake he felt he ought to do something about Imogen, and Imogen had said she couldn't possibly go without him, she wouldn't know a soul. He had happened to see Penelope a week or so before the party. She had been having lunch in the House of Lords with a peer he particularly disliked, a red-faced bucolic-looking ass whose only interest was in the breeding of racehorses and who was seldom seen in the House of Lords and never in the actual Debating Chamber.

Penelope had hurried over to talk to him with such enthusiasm that he almost forgot for the moment that he did not like her. She was astonishingly well preserved. She must be well over sixty by now and yet she maintained a genuine prettiness. Her hair was neatly waved and curled just as it had been in the thirties—dyed of course by now but well done, so that the ash blonde was only just disting-uishable from a possibly more appropriate grey—and her face had still a kind of pink and white softness about it.

She was wearing brown velvet and a pale pink blouse with some sort of scarf effect round the neck. She carried a little fur—sable probably—and diffused, but not too strongly, expensive scent.

'Such *years*—' she said. 'You know we saw darling Orlando quite soon before he died, looking so beautiful and young I couldn't believe it when I read it. I wish we could have a long talk.' She lowered her voice. 'Too boring, old Buffy, isn't he? But, my dear, we're in the racing world now. Guy's dotty about it. We must have a talk about the old days. Oh dear, Buffpots is blowing down his whiskers, I'd better go. Come to my party, now do, and bring that incredible Imogen. I saw her the other night—too beautiful for words—who's she going to marry?'

'She's still very young.'

'She was with the most terrible cad the other night. I don't know many young these days but the people I was with said he was no good at all. I've got several eligibles coming. Andrew Cathcart for instance. Now wouldn't that be suitable? A place, rolling in money, and too good-looking and sweet for words. Bring her along and I'll do the rest. He won't be able to resist her.'

Afterwards Conrad had thought that perhaps he ought to have done more for Imogen. It had not been enough to have once taken her to a Buckingham Palace Garden Party. Who else had she got to see that she met nice people and all that sort of thing? Agatha was no help. Of course match-making in Penelope Waring's blatant sort of way was quite ridiculous, but on the other hand if she did happen to take an interest in Imogen and introduce her to a few people, what harm could there be in that?

So they drove up together in a taxi to Wilton Crescent, both preoccupied by concerns very far removed from anything to do with Imogen's chances in the marriage market, though it was with this in mind that Conrad had not been able to repress a slight feeling of irritation at noticing that she was not looking her best. Her face was too pale and tense, lacking its usual serenity, and her constant fiddling with anything which could keep her fingers occupied, whether bracelets or pearls or the ends of her own hair, was even more noticeable than usual.

'I may have to leave you,' he said. 'There's rather a lot on.'

She looked at him as if she was afraid of having offended him.

'Yes,' she said humbly.

'One has to show a bit of solidarity,' he said defensively. 'I shall probably have to speak later on. I'm thankful I'm not in the Commons. Heaven knows what's happened to the level of debate in this Parliament. The Labour people descend to personal abuse in the most improper way.'

'Why are they so cross?'

'Cold feet. They were supporting Eden up to the hilt a day or two ago. Now suddenly they're squealing and talking about the United Nations. As if that could possibly do anything effective at this stage.'

'Is there a war on or something then? I mean, I haven't really read the papers.'

'Police action, that's all. Somebody's got to take a firm line.'

'Oh yes.'

'They blame the Government for not taking a firm enough line with Hitler—though no one would have supported a strong line at the one moment when it might have worked, right back in 1936 over the Rhineland—and then they complain when it does take a strong line with Nasser.'

'But I thought Nasser was in Egypt,' said Imogen, looking alert.

'Well, he is, yes,' said Conrad, rather taken aback.

'Anyway I'm sure you're doing the right thing, Uncle Conrad.'

'It's not up to me exactly. It's not my sphere, I can merely advise in general terms, put my point of view and so on, but my prime responsibility is not in foreign affairs or defence these days. The point is, though, that I have faith in my colleagues who do have the prime responsibility. There's such a thing as loyalty, you know.'

'Yes.' She ached from keeping still, from not running away, not crying out, not allowing herself to think. Two days of it she'd had. But loyalty. Loyalty meant standing by your sister even when you thought that what she was doing was rash, even wrong. Everybody knew what loyalty meant. But it would have happened anyway. The Inspector had said they'd known already that Agatha had had something to do with it. If something awful did happen, it would have been bound to have happened anyway. No one need ever know that she had had anything to do with it. If Agatha did know she would forgive her. I'm only quite young, she thought, getting out of the taxi; if I'd been older I'd probably have known what to do.

'Oh lovely, no, I adore champagne,' though it gives me a headache and I'm going to drink too much out of nerves. 'What a lot of people. Oh yes, I expect I do know some of them. I work on a magazine. Yes, it is, super fun. Oh no, not at all. Everyone's terribly kind.'

'—half-witted, I'm afraid. The sister's rather nice.'

They couldn't be talking about her, they couldn't. They wouldn't, not so close. There must be other half-witted people with rather nice sisters.

'—to be introduced to your beautiful niece—'

But he was a thousand years old, talking in terrifyingly level tones, his face much too close to hers. 'The Royal Family are an anachronism, don't you agree?'

'Oh *yes*. Well, except I did think the Coronation was rather super.'

'I expect you're part of the Princess Margaret set.'

'Oh *no*—'

'I don't think much of them, do you? Rather brainless, don't you agree?'

'Well, I don't know really, I mean they couldn't possibly be more brainless than I am. Are you someone terribly important?'

'I've been called one of the most acute financial brains in the City. It may be an exaggeration. That's how I came across our host. Wrong about everything else but right about money. Interesting, don't you agree?'

'Fascinating.'

'Your uncle's a very interesting man. He hasn't yet recognised that this country's a third-rate power. But he's very much respected. One of the most respected men in public life, don't you agree?'

Imogen agreed.

'. . . and Mr Carey the ruthless financier. You're not to
monopolise the prettiest girl in the room in your ruthless
financial way. Isn't she divine? She's turned down all the
most eligible men in London, Andrew, so it's up to you.
Come along now, Mr Carey, I'm going to find something
much more suitable for you.'

'I must say I do admire that sort of hostess, don't you?
It's rather gone out these days, that sort of thing.'

'Yes, I suppose so. It's a bit embarrassing though. I
don't think I've turned down any eligible men really. Anyway I never know whether they're eligible or not.'

'That's where someone like Penelope Waring is so useful. She tells you.'

'Yes, but she probably does it in front of them and that's
enough to paralyse anyone with shyness—'

'Where's your uncle, my dear? He's wanted on the
telephone.' It was Guy Waring, red-faced, ageing, finding
the party rather hard going.

'He's over there somewhere, I think. Yes, there. Oh
dear.'

'What's the matter?' asked the eligible young man.

'Uncle Conrad's wanted on the telephone.'

'Was he expecting some bad news?'

'Oh no. I mean perhaps he was. I don't know.'

'Are you sure you're feeling all right?'

'Oh yes, it's just—I think I'd better go and see what
it is.'

She began to push her way across the room. The
eligible young man watched her for a moment but his brief
spark of curiosity was quickly extinguished by the approach of an elegant married lady with a satisfactory little
scandal to relate.

By the time Imogen found her way to Conrad's side he

124

was talking to a fat man with a moustache—in fact the same peer with whom he had seen Penelope and whom he had been unable to avoid as he came back into the room after talking on the telephone.

'Splendid,' the fat peer was saying. 'Simply splendid of Anthony. As soon as I heard in the Club I sent him a case of champagne and an invitation to shoot. "The sort of leadership we need," I said on my card.'

'I don't suppose the Prime Minister has much time for shooting at the moment,' said Conrad coldly.

'Hasn't he? Is he not much of a shot then? Good Lord, hadn't thought of that. Don't want the fellow if he's not a decent shot. I mean, can't have him banging all over the place, can I, even if he is the Prime Minister.'

'I expect the problem will solve itself. I must be on my way.'

'Can I come with you, Uncle Conrad? I've got to go now too.'

'Don't you want to stay a little longer?' Not a success then, he thought. 'All right, I'll get you a taxi.'

As they walked out on to the pavement and into the cold dark air she said, 'Was it anything urgent?'

He put his hand under her elbow, guiding her towards Belgrave Square in search of a taxi.

'It was Skarrett. They think they're on to something. I'd asked him to keep me informed at every step. They think he's in Swindon. They're surrounding the house now.'

'Now?'

'He's going to telephone me at the House of Lords as soon as he has anything more to tell me.'

'Will you let me know? I'll be at the flat.'

'Yes. Don't worry. It will be a relief when he's caught. It will be over then.'

'Will it? I mean, yes.'

She could not talk about Agatha.

'Thank you for taking me to the party.'

'It wasn't very interesting, I'm afraid.'

'I don't think I really awfully like those sort of people.'

'I know what you mean. Some of them are all right of course.'

'Oh yes.'

'I suppose it's good for one to go outside one's own set every now and then. I have such a round of official dos, in official circles I suppose one would say. Official circles are very small.'

'Yes, I suppose so.'

'Anyway one certainly gathers that the vast mass of public opinion is solidly behind the Government over this Suez thing.'

'Oh yes, I'm sure it is.'

'Not that I suppose one could call that party the vast mass of public opinion. But they must be fairly representative.'

'Oh yes, they must be.'

He saw a taxi and waved to it to stop. When Imogen was inside he banged the door briskly and stepped back onto the pavement with a cheerful wave. She waved back, smiling palely through the window and the darkness. Poor little Imogen, he thought.

Paul was thinking that really the whole thing had been too much for him. He was terribly tired. In the grey cold morning light, waiting to show his forged passport and walk onto the boat which was to take him to freedom, he had no fear left, no nerves at all, was conscious of nothing but indigestion and an iron-grey sky. Overtired. Suddenly he remembered his mother sitting down on the sofa at Wood Hill, stretching out her long legs in front of her onto the stool with the tapestry seat which she had embroidered herself and saying, 'I'm a bit overdone,' and Orlando laughing and explaining that when you had been overdoing things you didn't linguistically speaking become overdone, like a piece of roast beef. But perhaps she had used the phrase often, that he should remember it so clearly, and her sitting on the sofa there and her shoes with their three straps which buttoned and her dark silk stockings, a striped jumper thing belted round the waist, the belt of the same material fastened with a small tortoiseshell buckle, a pleated skirt and the smell of her scent, always the same, always redolent of everything most longed for and most elusive.

'We'll get some coffee on the boat.'

They had said to talk naturally, going through the barrier, and besides he did not want to think about his mother. Indigestion, grey sky, that was all. Also a familiar, settled, inconsolable, uncomprehending, central grief; but he had never been without that.

Even when he saw the four tough-looking individuals waiting beside the two passport officials he thought nothing of it. It was not that sort of morning, everything so drab, so understated, not a morning for dramatics.

''Morning.' Neither cheerful nor uncheerful, secure in his blackened hair, his horn-rimmed spectacles. It was all organised.

Even when they said, 'Do you mind stepping this way?' he did not bother to look at his companion (one of them was travelling with him) for guidance or for reassurance. Obviously it was all meant to be like this, otherwise everyone would not be so calm; probably this was some prearranged manoeuvre to get them onto the boat as quickly as possible. He followed, firm steps, grey sky, into a grey room. And one of them began to speak, using words he had heard before, using his own name, and warning him that anything he said would be taken down and—

Even then he was only able half to take it in. The full extent of the disaster was more than he could absorb. This was something that had been arranged, and when it happened there was something that he had to do. That had been arranged too and when he did it everything would be all right. So he did it.

They had not been on the look-out for it. When he suddenly arched over backwards, at the same time giving way at the knees, as if an invisible rope round his neck had been pulled extremely sharply from behind him at the same time as a brutal knee had been shoved into the small of his back, they were taken completely by surprise. The two nearest to him moved towards him, then stopped.

The one who had been charging him said, 'Christ.'

They stood watching, shocked. He had done himself an incredible violence. He clawed the air with twisted hands, choking, then fell to the ground, eyes turning backwards into his head, a blackened tongue, foaming saliva turning pink. He breathed in retches, twisting to and fro on the dusty floor, jerking and mercifully slowing, quietening, mercifully still.

There was silence. They stood there, staring, as if afraid it all might start again.

'Swallowed something,' said one of them superfluously.

Having no telephone, Agatha received Paul's letter before the news of his death. It was Saturday. Conrad, who had been told what had happened by Inspector Skarrett early that morning, was in London, the political situation being such that for once he was unable to get away to Mount Sorrel for the weekend. Henry was to arrive by train later. He had said that he had to work late at the office and had therefore not been able to come down on Friday evening. He had never worked late at the office in his life, and Agatha assumed he was seeing Sally and was hurt that he had used such a corny excuse. In fact he was spending the evening with Joe, whom he had taken completely into his confidence: if Agatha were to be arrested he wanted to be able to present her with a complete plan, not only for her best defence but for the care of the children in her absence and even for what they should do on her release. He thought that Agatha was as yet ignorant of how close the danger might be, and preferred to leave her so and to discuss things instead with Joe.

So Agatha read Paul's letter alone, in the kitchen of the cottage, while the children played outside; and she went through all the emotions she usually did go through in any confrontation with Paul: irritation, impatience, disgust, as well as sudden optimism, amusement and affection. 'Imagine my joy,' he had written at the end. The phrase might have had an ironic tone, but she did not believe he had meant it like that, she believed he had written it in a burst of hope and excitement, a child on an adventure using words he had heard from a grown-up, creating an unintentionally comic effect. She found it very moving— 'imagine my joy'—poor Paul. Thinking of him as free, as having escaped, she could only wonder how he would manage, how he could possibly find the discipline to turn his fantasies into any kind of book, whether he would survive, whether he would take to drink.

Mrs Parker, pushing open the door unexpectedly, thought how pale she looked, and tired; she often did. Of course the family had all taken it hard, that wretched boy, anybody could have told them he would never be any good, getting himself sent to prison like that; and then her living in London with two children, she wouldn't like to do that herself, and a difficult husband maybe for all his charm, and then losing the little dog like that the other day, a shame.

'I've a message for you. I saw Bob in the village going to

drive up with it and I said, "You take me up to the top and I'll go on down with the message and then I can put in an hour or two down there, cleaning up and that." There's probably a bit of washing too, isn't there? I know what it is.'

'Don't bother, Mrs Parker. Aren't you busy?'

'He's out all day today. I don't mind giving you a hand. Saves me on Monday, doesn't it, if I come to have a clean-round when you've gone. Here I am putting on the kettle for a cup of tea anyway so there's no stopping me now. Oh and the message before I forget. Your uncle's coming down late tonight and he wants to see you tomorrow after ten o'clock church because he's got to go straight back to London.'

'Ten o'clock church,' Agatha repeated stupidly.

'First Sunday in the month, they're doing that now, I forget why. Anyway that was the message. Shocking, isn't it, him having to be away all the time like that. He never used to be away that much. Have a cup of tea yourself, why not? You look paler even than when I came in and I thought then you were looking tired. You remember Jen, Stephen's niece that looked after you?'

'Do you ever see her?'

'Ran into her in Marks and Spencer's in Bath last week. I don't often see her, she lives towards Cranmore, married a farmer, doing very well, she said. She certainly looked it. Three times the size she used to be.'

'Did she have children?'

'Four. Nearly grown up the boy must be. She had the little one with her, lovely little boy he was.'

'How old?'

'Six or seven. She was always good with children. Though I often think, nice as her own kids are, it was you got the real caring for. It's different when you're busy and got several. She'd nothing else to do when she was looking after you. We all noticed it. She was only a child herself really, but she'd have done anything for you.'

'Would she?' said Agatha, trying to imagine it.

'Not that she spoiled you. She was quite strict sometimes. You had to have nice manners and that. And when you had one of your temper tantrums she'd just stand there, that patient, and wait until you'd finished. Then you used to have to make it up with her. She wouldn't speak to you for a bit afterwards, it used to really worry you.'

'I remember her quite clearly, but not what she looked like. I suppose I was still very young when she left. I remember nothing but good things about her. All the happiness of my childhood really was with her. Except for sometimes when my father came and played with me. I was only her job. It was awfully nice of her to bother with me as much as that.'

'There was no one else bothering,' said Mrs Parker, who had never much cared for Agatha's mother. 'Anyway she was that sort. You get them like that sometimes, you can tell them anywhere.'

'Yes. Paul didn't have that. No one breathed the breath of life into him like that. He had that awful nanny.'

'That nanny,' said Mrs Parker happily, beginning to slosh about in the sink. 'Now she really was a shocker.'

Agatha usually enjoyed Mrs Parker's terrible tales about Nanny, but today they reminded her too strongly of Paul's troubles and of how early they had begun. On the pretext of needing to collect some firewood she went out of the house and, calling to the children to come with her, set off into the woods.

'When's Daddy coming?'

'Twelve o'clock. We'll go and meet him.'

'Can we go onto the platform and see the train?'

'Yes, if we're there in time.'

'Good.'

They ran ahead of her, forgetting they were supposed to be collecting wood.

'We're cowboys. I'm the captain and you're the sergeant.'

'I don't want to be the sergeant.'

'You can be the sergeant in command of the second rank.'

'I'm called Sergeant Bacon.'

'O.K. All troops advance NOW.'

'Second rank ADVANCE.'

'Sergeant Bacon, please take your men over there and form emplacements.'

'Second rank ADVANCE. Form PLACEMENTS.' Lucy skipped past Agatha. 'I'm forming placements,' she said, pausing to roll her eyes in a far from military manner. It was something she had just learnt to do; the effect veered between lunacy and extreme sophistication.

Sally cried, wanting to go to Hungary.

'In the first place I'm not going to Hungary,' said Joe patiently. 'It's impossible to get in. The roads from Austria have been closed.'

'You just don't understand me. You think I'd be in the way or have hysterics or something.'

'I think you'd be bored, that's all, and cold and uncomfortable.'

'Women can stand cold much better than men. It's been scientifically proved.'

'It may be all a false alarm. Nothing may happen.'

'Of course something's going to happen. All those tanks after they said they were withdrawing.'

'Here, have a hanky. I'll send for you, if it goes on. When I see what it's like.'

'I don't want to be sent for. I want to come with you. It won't go on. England and America will stop it.'

'How? They won't risk a world war.'

'Well, moral pressure or something.'

'What kind of moral pressure can we exert when we're doing the same thing ourselves in Egypt?'

'Oh Joe, how can you say that? It's quite different. We've got right on our side.'

'Oh yes, I forgot.'

'Please let me come. I want to prove myself. I want to bend over all those bleeding revolutionaries, deftly bandaging. Honestly I'd be so good at it.'

'There might not be any bleeding revolutionaries. They might not resist. Anyway, listen, there's something else. This is the real reason why I want you to stay here. I can't tell you why, and I don't want you to ask me or say a word about it to anyone else, but I think Henry might need some help soon.'

'Henry? Whatever for?'

'I said don't ask.'

'I hate mysteries.' But she dabbed her face half-heartedly with his handkerchief—the tears had left no trace—and leant back against the pillows of his bed. They were in his warm little room, drinking tea. 'Don't say Agatha's leaving him. He'll fall apart, you know.'

'That's not what you were saying a few days ago.'

'I thought I could take him on myself then. You changed all that. You completely changed my view of myself. It's a terrible responsibility for you. But I've always known he was hopelessly weak.'

'I didn't tell you that.'

'No, but he is.'

'I don't agree with you. I think that in some ways he's very strong. He has one of the strongest—I don't know what to call it—personal atmosphere, personality, I suppose—one of the strongest personalities of anyone I know. His trouble is that his father thinks he ought to be an

A.D.C. to the Governor General of Australia and won't realise that all that sort of thing is irrelevant, is fading away.'

'What a pity.'

'We're quite lucky, you and I, not to be more upper-class.'

'I think I am rather upper-class. I could pass as an aristocrat, couldn't I?'

He looked at her thoughtfully and then said, 'Not—quite,' which made her laugh.

'Besides,' he went on, 'that's different. To choose to be an aristocrat is quite different from being born one. We're coming to a time when everyone, including the aristocracy, is going to pretend the aristocracy doesn't exist. To choose to be an aristocrat at such a time is a thoroughly intelligent and amusing thing to do. You couldn't do it if you had been born one.'

'Really? Could I have done it if I had married Henry?'

'It would have been unutterably banal.'

'I adore you. I wish you would talk for ever. Which reminds me, I must go. I'm meeting Johnny. I'll ring you up later and let you know how it goes.' She stood up and reached for her coat. 'I'll look after Henry then, and you can look after the Hungarians, but not for long. You must come back quickly so that we can go on our jaunt to Paris and become terribly sophisticated.'

He saw her to the door and hurried back upstairs. Then he opened a drawer and took out the equipment which he had stuffed into it as Sally arrived: a sleeping bag, a box of medical supplies, tins of food and an empty haversack. Into this last he began to put a random selection of clothes. He was smiling. Sally in a Dormobile with five men. The imagination boggled.

Henry arrived on the evening train, bringing Imogen

with him.

As soon as she saw Imogen, Agatha knew that something had happened, but because she had brought the children with her to meet the train she did not like to ask what it was. It was only back at the cottage, when Imogen with slightly ostentatious helpfulness had hurried the children off for a bath and a really long story, that Henry was able to tell her about Paul's death.

Imogen was pleased to have something to do. As soon as she had heard what had happened, she had had a feeling of crisis—of Agatha, whether or not betrayed, needing her help—and a corresponding feeling of being able to cope, because at least she could cook, clean and look after the children. On the way down in the train it had suddenly seemed to her that all her life what she had really wanted to be was a nurse, and she had absolutely made up her mind that the minute the present crisis was over, and when she was quite sure that Agatha did not need her, she was going to start training. She would write off as soon as possible for details. She only hoped to goodness you didn't need School Cert. Maths to be accepted. In the meantime the resolution made gave her an unaccustomed feeling of stability.

'Instead of doing any good, I brought about his death,' said Agatha.

'You did it because you thought he couldn't bear life in prison. I don't think he could. I think he would rather have been dead.'

She brought out the letter and handed it over to him.

'It came this morning.'

Henry began to look through it, turning over the pages rather quickly, not liking the tone of it. It was too like Paul.

'He says at the end about the pill he had,' said Agatha.

Henry looked at the end of the letter.

'Poor Paul,' said Agatha as he read. She looked across at him reading and remembered what else came towards the end of the letter. 'He wrote something about us.'

She was determined to find some consolation other than the bleak consideration that he was better dead.

'He did a good thing. He sent me a really helpful message. Read it. About you and me and me being so bossy and you having to get away from me. Of course he's quite right. I am like that and I shouldn't be. That was a good thing he did, to tell me that.'

To Henry what Paul had written seemed neither true nor untrue, of no interest really, but he did not say so.

'Are they very quick, those pills, cyanide or something?' she asked.

'A few seconds, no more.'

They sat in silence on either side of the fire. They had never managed to get the lighting quite right in the sitting-room of the cottage; there was a lamp by which you could read if you sat beside it, but the rest of the room was shadowy except for the glow from the fire. Agatha felt that she loved Henry, with a love so detached as to be quite close to indifference and yet at the same time it was totally involved, the opposite of indifference. She breathed gently, hoping the feeling would not fade, and hoping he would not say anything, or move. Sometimes he spoilt things by what seemed to her a false gesture, a sentimentality. This time he did nothing. She added gratitude to the rest.

Conrad, coming into church late and preoccupied, hurrying up the aisle to his accustomed place in the front pew, was shocked to see Agatha and Henry standing side by side—the first hymn was just beginning—in a pew towards the back of the church. Immediately afterwards he was thoroughly annoyed to see the broad tweed-begirt backview of Daintry a little further up the church; he was not a regular church-goer—what on earth had possessed him to come today of all days? As for the effrontery of Agatha and Henry, whom he knew perfectly well to be heathens—Henry, what's more, if not Agatha, must certainly have a very good idea as to why he had asked to see her afterwards—the whole thing was extremely unfortunate and unpleasant, and, kneeling down for a moment before standing up to join in the hymn, he was so angry, that he muttered, 'Bloody cheek!', meaning it to apply to all of them. Fortunately there was no one near enough to over-hear. The church, as usual, was three-quarters empty—which made it worse of course, because when the time came for him to read the lessons he would have to face a congregation in which these three unwelcome faces would be unnecessarily obvious.

'Ransomed, healed, restored, forgiven,' he sang mechanically, thinking, Why should Agatha and Henry be here, what's their game, are they trying to curry favour?

In a way they were trying to curry favour, not so much by appearing in church as by not keeping Conrad waiting afterwards. If they were there, they ran no risk of misjudging the length of the service. They knew that Conrad would be going back to London as soon as possible. Indeed, having read in the morning papers that there were to be Cabinet meetings all day to deal with the Egyptian crisis, they had hoped he might have been prevented from leaving London at all. His presence showed them that things were serious. On that particular Sunday morning it was easy to believe. They both had indigestion. They both, at about the same moment, tried to remember whether Church always gave them indigestion. Neither retained the thought long enough to answer the question; but a truthful answer would in both cases have been in the negative; apprehension was the trouble, and the feeling, until then familiar to both only in the context of childbirth, of being caught in the current of inexorable events. Paul had swallowed poison; it seemed that in the streets of a town not known to either of them men and women were throwing themselves at moving tanks; it was to be expected that upon Agatha and Henry too some punishment should be visited.

Henry's anxiety was largely for Agatha, that she should be spared excesses of grief or anger, but he also dreaded the interview with Conrad on his own account because he was afraid of his father. He thought that Conrad probably knew about Agatha's part in Paul's escape and that the police probably knew about it too. He hoped that Paul's death would be seen to make any legal prosecution of Agatha unnecessary, but he was not confident. Presumably, however, it was for the police to decide whether or not to prosecute and he could not believe that Conrad was without influence on their decision. What he could believe very easily was that Conrad might exact some private penalty of his own, and that at very least there would be a lengthy scolding which would infuriate Agatha. But we are not children, he was thinking, we can go away, after this morning we need never see him again if we don't want to.

Conrad faced them to read the first lesson. The Vicar leant back in his seat behind him, stiffly because childhood polio had left him with both legs in irons and they were difficult to manipulate in the constricted space of a pew. Sunlight infiltrated; two pale shafts, in which suspended dust was slowly moving, fell onto two empty pews. Agatha, contemplating Daintry's back through one of them, allowed her thoughts to float, like the dust in the sunlight. Old Testament words sounded doom. Daintry's daughter Serena, Paul's wife, had married again, featured in a *Tatler* photograph and a feathered hat, petrified perhaps in both for ever, for Agatha had never seen her again.

Orlando had once told her that Daintry had said of Paul that he would sell his own grandmother even if he didn't need the money. It was in Italy that he had told her that, where their understanding had been so complete. I am only made, she thought, of what has been put into me by him, who for all his affection for Conrad would have been on my side now, so that I am only following on from him, and from the other mostly forgotten influences of my childhood which have given me the lens through which I focus, so that what surrounds me is not a disconnected blur but a system of signals; other people must see other signals, but I cannot change my lens now and I believe it is the one I would have chosen had I been able to choose. I can only focus as clearly as I can with what equipment I have and in the meantime and for no good reason I may suddenly be required to sing. But she could not remember the psalm and had no prayer-book, so sang 'Der der der' not very well in tune, causing Henry to look at her in surprise. The choir was weak and Daintry no singer; there was old Miss Harrison, catlike at the back, and a voice or two elsewhere, casual and behind the organ-beat, but Agatha was not concerned, thinking about truth and death. And Conrad faced them again, reconciled to a service which for him today was a form observed and no more. He knew he was in a bad temper, or, to put it another way, weighed down by worry—and going to church as often as he did he could hardly expect to feel close to God every time. He wanted to get through with it—Skarrett would be waiting after all—the sooner it was all dealt with the better, so that he could get back to London and his proper duties in this time of crisis, with the Press being utterly unreliable, and woolly left-wing intellectuals whining, and Gaitskell, thank goodness, making an ass of himself, but Bevan, one had to admit, doing the icy contempt bit really quite well. Just let them try, that was all, let them try, the ones who snap at our heels, worry our trouser-legs, yapping abuse, let them try to bear the responsibility, the weight, the incredible complexity of things which we honourable men to the best of our abilities lend our experience and skill towards trying to understand. Who says we're bloody perfect?

Closing the heavy Bible, he looked across the golden eagle's head of the lectern straight down the aisle at Agatha. Shame on you, he thought. Away on a stream of her own thoughts, she had caught only a word or two of what he had been reading and had swept them into her own flow to confirm her purposes. She answered his look with a serenely preoccupied gaze which by no means improved his mood. Henry, on the other hand, rising slowly to his feet beside her for another psalm thought, Christ, he's terrifying.

Daintry, also looking at Conrad, was thinking what a fine English gentleman he was. Daintry was in that sort of mood, benign, a little nostalgic, but full of confidence in the future. He had come to church because he wanted to have a word with the Vicar afterwards and he had not expected to see Conrad. He thought it splendid of Conrad not to give up reading the lesson in his village church because of other business to attend to. What an upright fellow he was, bit cold of course, not much of the old *joie de vivre*. That was what he himself had always had, *joie de vivre*, no one could deny that, and now, just as it was all beginning to go a bit stale, now that he'd got so much that he'd wanted, money, success, power, two stuffed tigers in his front hall, along had come good old Denise to make life worth living again.

This was the news he broke to Conrad outside the church as the sparse congregation filed out into the wintry sunshine.

'Congratulate me,' he cried. 'I'm getting spliced.'

'Congratulations,' said Conrad, preoccupied, looking gravely towards Agatha and Henry, who had joined them.

'Super girl, half my age, God knows why she's taking me on. Denise Cornwall-Cope, you probably know her, she's been around a bit. Lovely creature, my type, not too small, I can't take those skinny Audrey Hepburn types. Anyway I knew you'd be pleased. Tell me.' And as Conrad had already turned towards the path which led to his own house, gesturing to Agatha and Henry to come with him, Daintry took his arm and walked with him along it. 'This vicar, is he a fairly broad-minded sort of chap? We've both been married before and quite frankly a Registry Office is good enough for me, but Denise thinks she'd like a church wedding with all the trimmings. He'll do it, won't he?'

'You'd have to discuss it with him. He's very easy to talk to.'

'Put in a word for me, there's a good chap. He'll take it from you. And, after all, you know a good deal about my business morals after what we went through over those takeovers. A takeover of a family firm and still to be on speaking terms—a triumph I call that, a credit to both of us, what? Incidentally'—here he half-turned, reached out for Agatha's hand and drew her close beside him, tucking her arm under his, so that she and Conrad were borne forward together, reluctantly linked by his substantial form and followed by Henry, frowning—'I've written to you both. You'll get the letters. I was bloody sorry to read in the papers about Paul. Poor wretched chap. I liked him well enough, you know, in spite of everything. We got on very well at one time before he turned against me. He was just bent, that's all. But you couldn't help liking him at times. Rotten luck for you all. But don't forget you've got friends.'

They had reached the door into the Mount Sorrel

garden. 'Well,' said Daintry, letting go of both their arms, 'that's it then.' He suddenly gave Conrad a hearty thump on the back. 'Keep up the good work!' Conrad coughed, taken by surprise. 'Show those gyppos where they get off!' He lowered his voice. 'And if he wants anything—you know, new heating system, organ doing over—I did think of offering to do something about the legs, but it's a bit delicate—a new pair of calipers or something, they can do wonders with some of these new materials—so much lighter. Anway, see how it goes, what?'

They were through the door, and safe.

'He's very kind,' said Agatha.

Henry looked shocked.

'He's very able,' said Conrad distantly.

Henry groaned.

Conrad, extremely annoyed both by the groan and by the encounter with Daintry, led the way in silence down the path towards the house, in through the side door and across the passage into the library. The library windows looked out onto the entrance front. Conrad's black Rover was drawn up on the gravel with a police car beside it.

Conrad sat down at his desk and, looking at Henry, said, 'Inspector Skarrett is in the next room. He has come to arrest Agatha for conspiring to help Paul escape from prison. She will have to go with him.'

Henry turned perfectly white. His eyebrows, narrowed eyes, nose and mouth were sharp lines on his white face. Conrad's heart began to beat faster. Agatha, less disturbed than either, sat down on the arm of a chair, drawing her coat, which she had not taken off, close round her, her hands in the pockets.

'Why?' said Henry.

'Why?' repeated Conrad, as if astonished at his question. 'Because she has broken the law.'

'Paul's dead,' said Henry.

'What difference does that make?'

'It's all over. What point is there in going on with it?'

'Nothing alters the fact that she has broken the law. This is a criminal offence.'

'She gave someone some money. Nothing more than that.'

'She was part of a criminal conspiracy to pervert the course of justice.'

'You could get those charges dropped.'

'What are you saying?'

'You could use your influence to persuade the authorities not to prosecute Agatha.'

Conrad was silent for a moment. Then he said flatly, 'I would not do that if this were a parking offence.'

The lines on Henry's face seemed to draw together into a vortex of rage. Conrad thought, All his life, in spite of all I have done for, him he has caused me nothing but distress. He felt he could hardly bear the accumulation of agony.

'You have never understood.' He was trembling. All right then, if they wanted it like that let there be dramatics. He had been restrained too long. 'You young people have simply no idea of right and wrong. You are utterly and completely spoilt. What would happen if everyone were as irresponsible as you? If everyone broke the law when they felt like it? Don't you understand that without law, without rules, without loyalty to the law and obedience to the rules, everything collapses, falls apart? I am a Minister of the Crown, my prime loyalty is to the State. Paul was a traitor, the worst thing a man can be. Agatha made herself his accomplice. I gave her every chance, I sent her messages, by Imogen, by you, telling her to go to the police and stop fooling about. My duty is perfectly clear.'

'Duty?' began Henry.

Agatha stood up and held his arm before he could go

any further. She had hardly listened at first, had been sitting on the arm of the chair wondering whether she really felt as calm as she thought she did; but when their voices were raised she heard, and now said 'Don't,' feeling that she knew exactly what each would say and that it would be a mistake for them to say it. 'There's no point. You can't expect him to understand. He's different from us.'

'Of course I'm different from you. I have a sense of responsibility. I hoped Henry was going to develop one too, but I see that's quite impossible now.'

Agatha smiled. 'I haven't any influence over Henry, if that's what you mean. At least I don't think I have. And I have got a sense of responsibility too, only it's quite different from yours.'

'Evidently.'

'There are quite a lot of people like me, I think. I can see why you don't like us. We're not really on your side, you can't rely on us. We're a sort of underground, a subversive group.'

Conrad looked at her suspiciously.

'To us it's more important that someone's our brother than that he betrays his country. We're not even quite sure what that means, to betray one's country. It's like Paul said in his letter: you're always climbing up the ladder, that's your world, the ladder with rungs in it and everything according to the structure of rules which you've made, respect for the man who climbs the ladder fastest. But we're the opposite of that, we're in a river which flows both ways and has curves instead of straight lines and everything is flow and movement.'

Conrad and Henry were now both looking at her, Conrad with continued suspicion and Henry controlling a wish that she would shut up so that he could start shouting at his father. She was concentrated, not to be stopped.

'We may be anywhere, you see, that's our danger to you. We are worse than any organised revolutionary movement because you never know where one of us may turn up. We don't need to speak to each other. You could put me down in a street in China and I'd know which were ours, just by a turn of the head or a tone of voice. We are the real underground, we will never pay you honour or any of your gods, or judges, or policemen. We've been there always, an ancient alternative way you've always known about and always been afraid of. We're marked with it, we can't be anything else, we were kissed on the forehead in our childhood.'

'Mad,' said Conrad, drumming his fingers on the desk and half-turning towards the door behind which he knew that Skarrett was waiting, re-reading the paper probably, wanting to get on with the job and get back to London.

'Of course I'm not mad. You're not marked like us; your heart was broken when you were a child and reset to fit the pattern. That's why everything you do is just a little false. But when I was a child there was someone in the house from the other side, a girl no one noticed. Even I hardly remember her, but the harm was done, the imprint was made. She kissed my forehead and that's what I have to pass on to my children. To redeem them.' She turned to Henry. 'You know I talk in an exaggerated way, but it is the truth. It's even there in his own religion, but of course they took it over and made an institution, a Church— which incidentally has done more damage than most other institutions—but anyway it's even in that. There are so many diffcrent ways of saying the same thing—in fact most things are only different ways of saying the same thing because there are only a very few true things in the world. They come up in different forms and the difficult thing is recognising them, even when it looks as if they have nothing in common except a certain shape or a ratio

145

between the parts. We don't recognise correspondences. Anyway what I mean is—' She turned back to Conrad. 'It's even there in your own Bible, about abiding in love, you were reading it this morning. "His love is perfected in us." It's another language but it's saying the same thing.'

'Don't quote my own religion at me.' Conrad stood up slowly, leaning his hands on the desk in front of him. His voice was quite dry and cold. 'I shall call in Inspector Skarrett.' He took a few steps towards the door, then turned back to say in the same tone of voice, 'Do you think you have a monopoly of love, simply because you claim it was affection for your brother rather than malice which led you to commit a criminal offence?'

He did not wait for an answer, indeed turned quickly back towards the door into the next room so as to avoid one; but as soon as he turned Henry went over to Agatha, took her hands and said decisively, 'You're quite right. Absolutely right. Don't worry, we'll manage. Everything will be all right, do you understand?'

He dropped her hands as Conrad, having signalled rather imperiously to Inspector Skarrett that he might now enter, turned back into the room. Conrad saw Henry move away, stand by the window leaning his forehead against the glass, then briefly cover his face with his hands to conceal some sort of grimace. He's even going to cry, thought Conrad scornfully.

Henry was not crying, and the expression he was momentarily unable to control was one of foolish joy. He was tremendously excited, too excited to listen to Inspector Skarrett's level tones reciting his piece in the background. He seemed to have had a revelation, which was simply that Agatha was wrong. All his life he had taken it for granted that in all important matters, especially moral questions, Agatha was right, and that when he had diverged from her he had been wrong. He had assumed she was right when she started to speak to Conrad and as his own temper cooled and he began to listen he was full of admiration for what she was saying, which, while it had seemed wild and incoherent to Conrad, was immediately understandable to him because it was an expression of her way of looking at things and, as such, deeply familiar to him. She had started quietly but as she went on without much raising her voice she had become more vehement, swept into the stream of her own eloquence, beginning to gesticulate as she did when she was angry, and he had felt anxious lest she should go too far, lose her temper with Conrad, lose her advantage. Of course she did rage sometimes, had done it to him occasionally, beating her hands together for emphasis, stamping a foot. Like Lucy, who stamped both feet sometimes, partly from frustration at not knowing enough words—'you *always never* let me do *anything*'—who also danced, responded to music, ran, climbed and made incredible fantasies of which she said, 'It's true because I say so,' annoying George, who would say doggedly, 'It isn't so, Lucy, it isn't so.' And as he remembered George, he suddenly thought, with an extraordinary feeling of welcome for an understanding, that it was George who would save the world, because he knew exactly where he kept his second-best red pencil. Anyone can dance, he thought.

And then he knew that Agatha would be lost in a street in China, for all her goodwill, because a turn of a Chinese head, a tone of a Chinese voice, quite simply meant something different. It isn't so, Agatha, and though I love and honour your point of view it isn't mine, and it isn't the universal truth, and we are both right and I can look after everything perfectly well for a bit and you can plunge blazing into your next necessary experience, which is prison.

'There we are then,' said Miss Bannister, fastening up her cartridge bag. 'On the warpath.'

The cartridge bag had belonged to her father, Major Bannister, who in the years of his retirement in Hampshire had enjoyed a bit of pheasant-shooting when richer neighbours invited him. Her Service background was something Miss Bannister, a pacifist, did not mention: Miss Wickham knew about it and once or twice had ventured a sly reference to inherited officer-class attitudes which had not amused Miss Bannister; who had nevertheless a certain fondness for the cartridge bag, made of good leather, with the initials J.B. on the flap, into which she had been packing not ammunition but ham sandwiches, and as well as those a small silver flask, again inherited from her father and curved conveniently for his hip pocket, into which she had just poured a mixture of Nescafe and whisky.

'That should keep us going,' she said, patting the bag encouragingly, as if it had been a horse.

'Seems a horrible mixture to me,' said Miss Wickham, blowing her nose.

'It's seen me through some tougher times than this, I can tell you. I marched all the way from Jarrow on it in 1931.'

'I wonder if I ought to have put on my other shoes,' said Miss Wickham sadly.

'For heaven's sake—' said Miss Bannister, her irritation exacerbated by guilt, because she had not marched all the way from Jarrow. She had joined the march rather more than half-way down its route. 'Let's go.' But as they were on their way through the front part of the shop—they had met there, although it was a Sunday, as part of a complicated subterfuge to avoid Miss Wickham's Empire Loyalist neighbours, with whom she had been meant to be having lunch, and who had had to be duped with tales of a sudden urgent need for stocktaking—the door was opened in a hurry and Henry came in.

'I thought you might be here,' he said. 'I rang both your numbers and got no answer, so I thought I'd walk along and see. Agatha's been arrested.'

Now that one could never be Viceroy of India, Conrad thought, perhaps there was no longer any point in going into public life. All that having come to an end with those really rather undignified photographs of Lady Mountbatten kissing Nehru, where was the satisfaction, what could anyone look forward to as a glittering prize?

This was what he was thinking as he sat in a smoky room, feeling rather than hearing the repeated and re-repeated arguments passing from side to side around him. He had heard them all before, but there was no alternative to sitting through it, whereas if the world had not changed so inordinately during his life time he might have had a perfectly good chance of ending up as Viceroy. He knew he would have made a good Viceroy. Instead, here he was as really quite an insignificant Cabinet Minister. He was respected, of course, had certain things to his credit, certain little fields he had made his own and in which he contrived to make a small effect; he was consulted on this and that, was supposed to have an influence on the party followers, to be admired in the constituencies; but he knew perfectly well that he would never be one of the inner sanctum. Nor was this only a result of the difficulties inherent in being a member of the House of Lords rather than the House of Commons. They think of me as a harmless old steady, he thought, a bit of a trimmer. Once he had been walking along the corridor in the House of Commons and as he approached a group of three of the younger M.P.s who were talking together he thought he heard one of them say, 'Here comes old oil-can,' and then they had all moved away. He could not be sure of it, and besides he had once heard that phrase used to describe one of his colleagues, and another Cainbet Minister, and so perhaps even if they had said it they had not been applying it to him. All the same he had wondered.

And wondered now what was the point of it all. Anything that was achieved was always so different from the idea's inception, was always brought about by such a curious combination of circumstances and pressures, mixed motives and muddled reasoning. It was hard not to be cynical, harder still as one grew older to find anything or anybody one could support without many reservations.

Yes, he would do his best to reassure the back-benchers, to still the critical tongues within the party. Of course he would, they knew him. But there were sounds now from outside, sounds he had not heard for many years, distant but recognisable sounds of an angry crowd, then horses' hooves, then booing. Disgusting, he thought.

The first fire-cracker to explode near her feet nearly frightened Miss Wickham out of her wits. She had been trembling a bit anyway from excitement and cold, and now clung to Henry's arm in panic until she saw the youth who was throwing the squibs and decided that he did not look as if he had a bomb in his other pocket. She was wrong in this but had let go of Henry's arm by the time she found out. The bomb was a smoke-bomb and, thrown with a quick sideways flick of the hand, it travelled far and fast to within a foot or two of the watching policemen. Through the resulting smoke two of them ran towards the youth, who dodged them and ran back into the crowd.

'Look out!' cried Miss Wickham excitedly, though it was not clear to whom she was shouting. But Henry put a hand on her arm and said, 'Come on, we're going this way.'

'Where to?' asked Miss Wickham.

'Downing Street,' answered Miss Bannister firmly.

150

Miss Wickham was impressed, not only by the firmness but by the matter-of-fact tone. Miss Bannister, in her tweed jacket and with her cartridge bag slung on her shoulder, had very much the air of an old hand at this game. The crowd among which they found themselves was predominantly youthful, sober on the whole, not noisy, but young. Miss Bannister had a certain authority. It was Miss Bannister who said, 'Downing Street' as the speeches came to an end and some members of the crowd began to wander away towards Leicester Square or Charing Cross in the tame pursuit of underground trains or buses to take them home to a late tea. That was not how rallies in Trafalgar Square had ended in Miss Bannister's young days.

She was evidently not alone in her resolve because there was a definite movement towards Whitehall—a surge, Miss Wickham told herself. The crowd surged towards Whitehall, she thought as if it were already written in the history books, feeling herself part of the surge, part of a great green mounting wave that was going to break on the bastions of power and change the course of events for ever. Caught up in the course of history, she thought.

'It's terribly exciting,' she said to Henry (not to Miss Bannister because she knew Miss Bannister would have thought her naive).

Henry looked at his watch.

'I did say I'd meet Imogen and the children,' he said.

He had found the demonstration interesting rather than exciting and would have liked to slip away. He had gone to see Miss Bannister and Miss Wickham ostensibly to tell them that Agatha would not be coming to work in the bookshop the following day, but really because, having driven Imogen and the children back to London, he had felt the need for activity, a desire to do something constructive towards the improvement of the situation. It being Sunday, there was very little he could do. He had telephoned Joe, but he had already left for Hungary, and Sally, but she was away for the weekend. He had managed to get hold of David Williams, the solicitor, and had arranged with him to approach the barrister they had already decided on as the best person to undertake Agatha's defence at her trial. Then he had gone in pursuit of Miss Bannister and Miss Wickham and had found them about to set off for Trafalgar Square.

There had had to be a pause for explanations, because they had not even known that Paul, whose case they had read about, was anything to do with Agatha, who had a different surname, but once they had been told the whole story and had expressed at some length their sympathy and support, they too were frustrated by the absence of scope for immediate action. Not only was Imogen with the children, but Willy, the Dutch girl, had already moved in to help. The next day Agatha was to appear in front of a magistrate to be committed for trial. They could be there, in court, but until then it seemed that the only thing to do was to go after all, a little late, to Trafalgar Square.

Henry went with them. He was not interested in politics and had been too occupied with other concerns to pay much attention to what he had read in the papers about events in Egypt; but when Miss Bannister told him that they were going to a rally to support a campaign for 'Law not War' it did seem that there was something to be said for her point of view. In fact, when one came to think of it, it was odd that England should be dropping bombs on another country without having declared war, and then there was also the fact that if one happened to hear Anthony Eden on the wireless it was a strangely embarrassing experience; and so for these reasons, and because he thought it would please Agatha and annoy his father, Henry had gone to Trafalgar Square. Miss Bannister and

Miss Wickham were both very pleased at the thought of having made a convert.

After the rally, though, he would have liked to leave. He had promised to meet Imogen and the children on the bridge in St James's Park at six o'clock, and though it was only just after five and rather cold he would rather have wandered off in that direction than become involved in a march on Downing Street. He could not feel himself to be that kind of person. The meeting had been one thing; he had been perfectly happy to be part of the crowd there. He had not been able to share Miss Wickham's emotion about Anthony Greenwood in his red tie. 'Who *is* he?' she asked, in breathless admiration. 'Tony Greenwood of course,' Miss Bannister had answered as if she had known him all her life, and indeed perhaps she had—but Aneurin Bevan's voice was so clear, so light yet carrying, so musical, that it was impossible not to listen to what he said, and what he said seemed sensible, and when he drew the conclusion that Anthony Eden was too stupid to be Prime Minister, his voice rising to an almost comical squeak of indignation on the word 'stupid', Henry clapped vigorously and shouted out, 'Quite right!' That, he now felt, should be the extent of his demonstration; but Miss Bannister had forged ahead through the crowd and he was left with Miss Wickham, who was in a state of hopeless over-excitement and really, he felt, not capable of looking after herself.

'Now let's just see if we can find Miss Bannister,' he said, hoping to pass on the responsibility.

But Miss Bannister was somewhere ahead, and they were obliged to follow the stream of people moving out of Trafalgar Square and into Whitehall, bunching up closer together as the police, of whom there now seemed to be an infinite number and in a very much less relaxed mood than they had been earlier on, hemmed them in, preventing them from moving out sideways, alerted perhaps by those few smoke-bombs and fire-crackers to a possible change in the temper of the crowd. A young man with a long football scarf round his neck stepped out of order to try to pass the people in front of him. A policeman seized him by the shoulders and pushed him roughly back into the crowd.

'Beast!' hissed Miss Wickham.

The policeman, who had not spoken during the incident, looked at her thoughtfully.

'Hush,' said Henry, feeling foolish and hustling Miss Wickham past. He was no physical coward, had even been rather good at boxing at school, but he was not at all sure that he could control Miss Wickham, and felt he could hardly be expected to take on the entire police force in her defence.

'Where on earth is Miss Bannister?' he said, trying anxiously to see over the heads of the crowd in front of him.

Conrad came out of his meeting with a headache. There was to be a full Cabinet meeting in an hour's time. What a lot of talk. It was clear that the Prime Minister was in an appalling state of nerves, and it was not clear that the military organisers were going to make the action the short sharp affair it had to be in order to succeed. He had walked to Downing Street from his flat and so had no official car waiting for him. Concerned with his thoughts and vaguely thinking of getting a taxi, he had walked a little way towards Whitehall before he noticed that the end of the street was barred by police horses and that the crowd noises which he had been hearing from inside the meeting were a good deal louder and more menacing than before. There was chanting—'Eden must go, Eden must go'— some angry shouts, and the sound of the horses' hooves as they moved to and fro, evidently rebuffing some kind of advance. He could see that beyond the line of mounted police there were more policemen on foot, shoulder to shoulder, and beyond them another line of mounted police. Suddenly a loud ragged booing began, rose almost to a roar and then died down. The attempted advance had failed and the crowd were expressing their disapproval of the police action.

Two of the policemen who had been standing outside 10 Downing Street had followed Conrad to advise him to go round the other way. He said he would, but paused a moment, still looking towards Whitehall.

'It shouldn't go on much longer,' one of the policemen said. 'They're beginning to clear off already.'

But at that moment there was a sudden disturbance, more shouts and clattering hooves, and a tiny spearhead of demonstrators broke through one side of the first rank of mounted police and pushed back the foot police, who momentarily wavered but then stood firm again. One of them lost his helmet and over his head there reared up— was she standing on something, or being carried?—the excited upper half of a small middle-aged lady.

Conrad had already half turned away to go back up the street, but the appearance of what might be supposed to be the leader of the mob was so unexpected that he paused to stare, and saw the frail form more or less thrown over the head of the policeman by a huge bearded man who now appeared behind her, struggling with the two policemen who had set upon him at the very moment when he had launched Miss Wickham into the air. From behind this struggling group there now appeared another dishevelled figure, who dashed up to where Miss Wickham, unbalanced by her unexpected leap, was picking herself up from the road, meanwhile in imminent danger of being trampled on by a police horse. Conrad recognised Henry. He heard his voice.

'Miss Wickham! Miss Wickham!'

But Miss Wickham was on her feet and hurling herself at a mounted policeman. Clinging tenaciously to a leather boot, she had for the first time an uninterrupted view of Downing Street, of one or two policemen looking infuriatingly calm and a bowler-hatted figure whom she did not recognise.

'Look out, we're coming,' she shouted to them rather as if it were hide-and-seek and she had just counted up to fifty.

'Miss Wickham!' cried Henry desperately.

Now she clasped a serge-covered thigh, her two feet firmly planted against the horse's side.

'Come on, Henry,' she shouted, wig awry. 'Up and at 'em!'

Aghast at the state of affairs seemingly revealed by the familiar use of the Christian name, Conrad watched in horror as Henry, held back by two policemen, struggled to reach Miss Wickham's side. The mounted policeman next to the one who was the object of Miss Wickham's attack, perhaps disconcerted by the frail aspect of his opponent, took off his glove before reaching over to try to pluck her from her perch. She bit him. He withdrew his hand sharply to put on his glove again, giving her time, still clinging to her victim like a tigress to an elephant, to shriek down the street as loudly as she could to the bowler hat. 'Eden must go! Down with imperialism! Down with the British Empire!' And then it was down with Miss Wickham, into a sea of dark uniforms, and down with Henry and down with the bearded man, and the dark uniforms realigned themselves and the shouting died down, but not before Conrad had turned away, white-faced, and walked towards the other end of the street.

'Only a few fanatics,' said the policeman who was walking beside him.

'One of them was my son,'

Conrad never failed to greet the policemen on duty as he passed them. He even took his hat off to the cleaners.

The policeman was sincerely shocked.

'I'm very sorry to hear that,' he said.

Imogen had taken the children to the Zoo. She had been about to set off when Henry had come back to tell them that he was going to the demonstration with Miss Wickham and Miss Bannister, and what with one thing and another it had been agreed that she should have the van for the Zoo expedition but should pick Henry up after his demonstration to drive him home. He could of course have gone home by bus, but Imogen felt that she wanted to keep the children in a constant state of activity in case they should start to worry about Agatha, and the idea of parking the car and running in the dark (because it would be already dark) across St James's Park to the bridge where they were to meet had appealed to them, as she had known it would. And now, excited by the darkness and the lights and the reflections in the water, they were running about and chasing each other and hoping Henry would not come too soon so that they could go on playing, and Imogen was waiting by a lamp-post, walking slowly up and down to keep warm and listening to the faint but rather disturbing sounds that were coming from the direction of Whitehall and wishing that Henry would hurry up.

She was glad to see the children playing. A few minutes ago in the car there had been a rather awkward little conversation about whether Agatha was coming to say goodnight to them or not. The trouble was that though they appeared to understand exactly what had happened it was as if they kept forgetting. Agatha had been taken to see them before driving away with Inspector Skarrett and had left them solemn but reassured. Had Grandfather said she was to go, they had asked, knowing of her appointment with him. Yes, she had said, because you were not really allowed to help people get out of prison, but Paul had been very unhappy there and had asked her to help him and you have to help your brothers. 'But you said prison was nice!' And in a way she had, trying to reconcile them to Paul's having been sent there; so she had had to explain that she had not meant that it was nice so much as bearable, for people who liked being alone, and reading, and writing long letters every single day to their children. And they had more or less understood, and had not cried until after she had gone, and then not very much, because Henry and Imogen had been there; but an impression had been quite definitely left on their minds—and Henry, in his present mood, had done nothing to change it—that the whole thing had been by decree of their grandfather, who was the most important person they knew.

So that when, in St James's Park, they suddenly saw him walking slowly out of the darkness into the lamplight, his hands in his overcoat pocket, his bowler hat pulled down over his forehead and his white face set into an expression of extreme severity, they were considerably shocked. His looks seemed to confirm his changed state, from the benevolent if sometimes alarming grandfather from whom, if you remembered to be on your best behaviour, perfectly good presents could quite frequently be expected, to something altogether different, infinitely more distant and cruel.

They stopped in front of him, drew closer together, stared.

He stared back, at first completely taken by surprise and then, as he realised their proximity to the scene he had just been witnessing, horrified. Had Henry completely lost his senses? Was he not only involving himself with a rabble of left-wing fanatics, but trying to bring his children into it as well?

'What are you doing here?' he asked them sternly, frowning at them as they confronted him under the lamp-post.

Lucy bent on him her most terrible gaze. He was the man who had sent away her mother.

'You are a—' she began ferociously but stopped. She had been going to say 'pig' but that was something she very often called George when she was cross with him and she needed a more frightful word. 'You are a SHEEP!'

Imogen had hurried towards them, seeing what was happening, and now stood beside the children, aligning herself with them but uncertain what else to do.

'Take them home at once,' he said to her. He walked away without looking back, but not so quickly that he did not hear Lucy's foot stamping furiously on the tarmac path. Her voice came after him, shrill but without a tremor in it, like an antique pipe.

'As long as I live!' she shouted. 'As long as I live!'

Agatha was in darkness, surrounded by stone. She was breathing in and out, very deeply and very fast, as she had learnt to do in labour. They had said then, 'Don't resist it, go with it,' but it did not seem to work when the pain was mental. She gave up, curled over until her head was on her knees, and hardly breathed at all. She was in a deep well, drowning in anxiety.

When Lucy had a temperature she walked in her sleep, pursued by monsters. Henry never woke. When George was late for school his legs, plump in their thick grey socks—had she mended them, did he need new ones?—pounded on the concrete playground their message of shame—shame—'Your mother's in prison,' they would say. Because she sacrificed your peace of mind to her selfish brother, who anyway was caught and killed himself.

'Think of Italy,' Henry had said, 'think of Italy.' But

she could not remember it. He had said they would go there afterwards; he would give up his job, they would work the land, cultivate the vines and the olives, the children would go to an Italian school, he would teach them English history himself in the evenings. It had made her laugh at the time because it sounded so unlike him. They were still both in the curiously euphoric state that had come upon them immediately after the arrest, as if the smell of burning boats in their nostrils were slightly intoxicating, removing all appetite for food but making the heart beat faster.

But by the late evening the euphoria had fled, to be replaced by fear. Obediently she tried to think of Italy but her thoughts would not settle. They dispersed in fragmented worries. The children. A bruise she ought to stop herself from fingering. Italy. After all had it not been paradise to her mind's eye all this time? Her paradise, though, hers and Orlando's. Was Henry to apply himself to it, make it his? That stony terrace on which Orlando had fallen, crushing the wild marjoram in the sacred noonday heat, must be ploughed up, the weeds must be poisoned, the snakes must slither away to more secret places, corn must be sown between the vines. Of course that was good, and good that the lazy hare should no longer have the ruined chapel to himself and good that the grass should be cut round the stone well and the tower house finished and the convolvulus destroyed. Would any of it be any concern of hers? She had first to be tried and condemned.

Henry had said, 'We'll come back, we don't want to be exiles.' But I am an exile already, she thought. Perhaps I shall always be an exile. People don't recover from being in prison, you can always see it in their eyes. Sally and Joe. Henry had said Sally and Joe could come to stay in Italy, they were friends now. How could she be expected

not to mind that a little? Joe was her old friend. Sally was—
but how after prison could she face Sally, or anyone else
like her? You had to be strong for all that, and strong for
marriage, for growing out of being in love, for accommo-
dating differences, for not minding being sometimes bored,
irritated, misunderstood, misjudged. How could she and
Henry stand up to the emphasis which would be given to
their relationship by going to live in isolation in Italy?
Leave it to him, he had said. But she had always had to do
all the worrying before. Wasn't that one of the reasons
why so much of the strength she needed now had been
used up? She had reached her limit, that was all. Sooner
perhaps than most people. What had they said in her
school report? 'She contributes nothing.' That was it. 'She
is too reserved. She contributes nothing to the life of the
school.' They can always get me that way. Remind me of
school and I'm alone in the narrow well of my own
inadequacy. What use are the woods to me now, wild
garlic and mud, the waterfall? How weak all that is. If I
live to be a hundred I will never dare to tell the children a
fairy story again.

Think of Italy, he had said. Dream it, dream Italy.
After all, she might sleep.

She thought of fallen stones by cypress trees, distance,
silence, stars, the snake among the tangle of brambles and
wild roses, the path from the wood along which for some
mythological purpose of her own she had once imagined a
unicorn picking its way between the stones. She might
sleep. Even in this well she might sleep and be restored.
And there had come into her mind the other place, the
place on the island which she could never be certain
whether she had seen or not, with the grass growing
between the white columns and the sea far below, and she
thought, There is a space between two broken columns, I
will make up a story about that and send it to the children.

161

In the sunlit space between two broken columns I will place a unicorn so that I may remember him. That at least she could do.

The bearded man was arrested and taken away.

'May I have a word with you, officer?' Henry said in the grandest possible tones.

He walked away a few paces with the senior police officer.

'Most awkward,' he said confidentially. 'My father's secretary. My father's Lord Field, I don't know whether you knew that. This lady has been his secretary for many years and is most devoted. We were just trying to make our way through to the House of Lords when that great big fellow suddenly seized her and started carrying her along. I'm afraid she became quite hysterical, poor thing. I don't know why she was shouting like that. I rather think she thought he'd do her some violence if she didn't pretend to be on his side. You can see she's in a severe state of shock. I really think I should take her straight home and get someone to put her to bed with a couple of aspirin.'

'She did appear to be assaulting a police officer, sir.'

'I'm afraid she was quite hysterical at that point. You can imagine what a ghastly experience it would be for someone like that, officer, after years of sitting quietly in Kensington typing letters for Cabinet Ministers. She was out of her mind with terror. There are a lot of very distinguished people who can vouch for her character. Perhaps if we left our names and addresses?'

The police officer stifled his doubts. He had a lot on his hands, and Henry's air of authority was very convincing. He didn't want any trouble about wrongful arrest. He took out his notebook.

'If you'll take the responsibility of getting her away from

here as quickly as possible.'

'I'll see to it, officer.'

The policeman wrote down the names and addresses of Henry, Miss Wickham and Miss Bannister.

'She's lucky to get away with it,' he said.

'Thank you very much, officer, it's very good of you,' said Henry, grander than ever. He gave a nod which was meant vaguely to imply that he would mention the incident to his father and make sure that the man was properly rewarded; then he led Miss Wickham and Miss Bannister firmly away.

Miss Wickham was beginning to wonder whether she had made a fool of herself. She was white-faced and silent, and could hardly walk for exhaustion. Miss Bannister, however, was still full of fight.

'Disgraceful,' she said as they walked away. Luckily the policeman had already turned back towards the noisy crowd. 'Sucking up to that policeman like that. Felicity should have seen it through and stood trial.'

'No, really, Miss Bannister, we can't have everyone in prison, now can we?' said Henry. 'Comfort yourself by thinking how it would annoy my father if he knew how we'd used his name.'

'I think I can probably be more use to the dear children if I'm at liberty,' said Miss Wickham faintly through colourless lips.

Conrad drove home through the night. He could not forget Lucy, that blazing look, that 'sheep!' The absurdity of the chosen term of abuse only made the insult more bitter. It showed how hard she had had to try to find a word bad enough to describe him.

Mount Sorrel was all he had now. He wanted to get back to it, to sleep there that night, even if it meant driving straight back to London in the morning. At night, with nothing much on the roads, it took him two and a half hours. He had often done it.

'It's all I've got,' he said aloud in the car. 'Everything else they've taken away from me.' His voice shook. He sobbed. Why not? There was no one to hear. 'My son. They've taken my son.'

He had telephoned before leaving London to find out what had happened. When Henry had answered the telephone he had said, 'Are you all right?'

'Why do you ask?' Such coldness.

'I heard—that's to say, I saw you were involved in a demonstration.'

'You saw?'

'I was coming out of Downing Street.'

'I see.'

'That woman—the woman you were with—who is she?'

'Agatha works for her.'

He might have known it. It would have been Agatha. Agatha worked for a left-wing organisation and was trying to draw Henry into it too. All her life she had been pulling Henry away from him.

'Henry, we haven't really had a chance to talk. About Agatha, I mean. Of course we must see that she has the best possible defence.'

'Thank you, Father. I have already seen to that.'

'Oh you've got somebody, you mean? Who have you got?'

'A man called Lindon.''

'I believe he's excellent, couldn't be better. If I can help in any way, financially or anything?'

'No, thank you, Father.'

'Now look here, Henry, I don't want this to come between us. We really mustn't let that happen.'

'It has happened, Father.'

'No, Henry, I'm not going to allow you to say that. You're my only son. Just because your wife and I don't agree over something. . . .'

'I think Agatha's right.'

'You can't let her ruin everything between us, after all I've done for you. You're the only thing I have left to remind me of my wife. No, no, this won't do, Henry. You are not as hard-hearted as that. I shall ring off now but you will think better of this. You will see that your attitude is wrong.'

'Yes I may,' said Henry in the same detached voice. 'But not yet. I really think it would be better if we were not to meet for the time being.'

After that he had had to get back to Mount Sorrel. What else was there? He had had to drive with limbs aching with tiredness—he was not young any more, did anyone ever think of that?—through the night towards the West, haunted by those scornful eyes, that confident cry of the child against the dark, 'As long as I live! As long as I live!' Imogen should have smacked her, told her she was a naughty little girl, instead of standing there doing nothing, looking as if she agreed with her. After all he had done for them all, it was hard to take in, hard to believe.

'Alexandra, they don't understand us any more.' But she was in a tennis dress, in 1929. Had she ever existed? Had he? 'Your heart was broken when you were a child, and reset to fit the pattern. That's why everything you do is just a little false.' Splinters of ice into his heart. Did she think his blood was too thin to flow like any other wounded creature's? No one had said that sort of thing to him before. It was simply not a recognisable picture. He was Conrad, wise, kind and just. Everyone else thought so. She knew nothing about training, about discipline and duty, just as she knew nothing about politics or government. You had to have different spheres of action, otherwise rational existence was out of the question. There was a sphere for private faith and a sphere for public duty, a sphere for the heart's affections and a sphere for the great world of affairs. They had to be kept separate, in an orderly and disciplined manner, if stability were to be maintained. What she was asking for was chaos, anarchy. Why did she have to speak as if she alone knew what impulse had first stirred the inert primeval slime?

Phrases circulated in his head. 'A broken man.' 'Nothing to live for.' There was humiliation for his country. The Government had bungled their Middle Eastern policy. What could he have done? Nothing. Over this particular issue the Cabinet had been kept in the dark by one small group. There was nothing left for him but loyalty. He was loyal, but not in sympathy. It was the inefficiency rather than the policy itself which seemed to him so disastrous. Eden was ill, would have to be replaced. He could not believe there could be a Conservative Government for much longer. By the time they got back he would be too old and would have come too badly out of the present situation to be given office again. If he was offered it he would refuse it. A man who had so completely lost heart should give way to someone else. Anyone else. Except a Socialist of course.

All that was over, those years of being always there, always somewhere near the seat of power, a constant influence. As long ago as before the war some newspaper had called him the youngest ever elder statesman. Now that he was old enough for the part he was going to lose it.

There were no lights on in the house as he drove up to it. He had had a Spanish couple, but the housekeeping bills had been so enormous and full of such inexplicably mysterious entries that he had asked them to leave and now had a complicated system of part-time help from the village, which worked quite well but meant that no one except Conrad himself slept in the house at night.

Getting out of the car, he stretched his arms and

breathed deeply, as he always did when he arrived at Mount Sorrel, then he stood in front of the portico for a few moments in the darkness and silence. A car passed, somewhere up the valley, and the silence returned. He took the key from his pocket and opened the front door.

As soon as he had turned the lights on in the hall he looked towards Orpen's picture of Alexandra. He always did. Before the war, when he used to travel a lot on Government Commissions and things of that kind, he and Henry used to go together to look at the picture whenever he came back from being away. It was a brief formality— 'Come on, let's go and look at Mummy,' the little boy would say, pulling him by the hand, wanting to get it over so that they could go on to other things, present-giving perhaps or stories of Conrad's adventures in distant parts of the world. They would stand there for a minute hand in hand, looking up at her as if to receive a blessing from the direct gaze inherited from the Field-Marshal and captured so brilliantly by the artist. She was in a garden party outfit. The gaze came from beneath the wide brim of a pale straw hat, which had a ribbon round it, tied in a huge bow at the back. The dress, of some light material in pale and less pale mauve, left the arms bare. Only one arm was to be seen because the artist had chosen a three-quarters view. She sat on a stool, one leg crossed over the other, one hand resting lightly on her hip, a pose which somehow showed her for the woman of action she was. The arm was beautifully painted, lightly dimpled round the elbow, turning inwards at the wrist so that the hand might rest on the mauve material, two fingers just catching the long strand of pearls, his wedding present. The hair beneath the hat was dark and curly, the cheeks a healthy pink, the nose not inconsiderable. The mouth, firmly closed, was a little amused at the corners. Altogether a handsome woman. What would she have made of it all, nearly thirty years later? She had been so honest, so simple and so brave. He tried to remember her voice, the words she used, words from a vanished world, a world where it was decent to be polite to servants and jolly to ride to hounds. It seemed much more than thirty years ago.

He heard a sound behind him, a soft sound as of slippered feet moving slowly across the stone floor. He had an instant of fear, knowing himself to be the only person in the house, but turned and saw Jess coming slowly towards him wagging her tail. Sleep, age and illness were making her drag her feet.

'Oh Jess, poor Jess, did I wake you up then?'

She hated sleeping anywhere but in the house unless she was with him, and the closeness of the house to the village meant that someone could come in in the evening to let her out and then leave her in her basket for the night. He had not been taking her to London with him lately because of her health, and as soon as he saw her he recognised that it had again deteriorated. She was moving badly and her breathing was even worse than when he had last seen her. He crouched down on the floor to receive her welcome.

'Even you, Jess, even you.'

His sorrow became uncontrollable, and he cried. The phrase 'he wept like a child' came into his head. Had he cried like that when Alexandra died? He could not remember. He wept like a child. Jess licked his face.

'Jess, poor Jess, you smell awful. Awful, Jess. You smell of death, I suppose, poor Jess. Perhaps I do too. I wish we could die together. We're no good here. We've got everything wrong, Jess, everything wrong.'

He wept into her soft neck, crouched on the floor beside her in his London overcoat. At last, exhausted, he lay down. She pressed herself against his side. He turned towards her and they lay together on the stone floor, her head resting on his. Mrs Benjamin, the first of the helpers, would find them. 'There they were together on the floor, cold the two of them, stone cold.' Wouldn't they be sorry even then? Perhaps it didn't matter. It was not for that that he wanted to die but because he was finished, destroyed. He prayed, 'O God, let me die.'

'O God, let me die.'

His prayer was not answered. Much later he went upstairs and got into bed.